ILLUSIONS
OF HAPPINESS

SCARY SHORT STORIES

ILLUSIONS OF HAPPINESS

SCARY SHORT STORIES

ERIKA LANCE

4 Horsemen
Publications, Inc.

DEDICATION

To Val – It's a good thing you are pretty.

TABLE OF CONTENTS

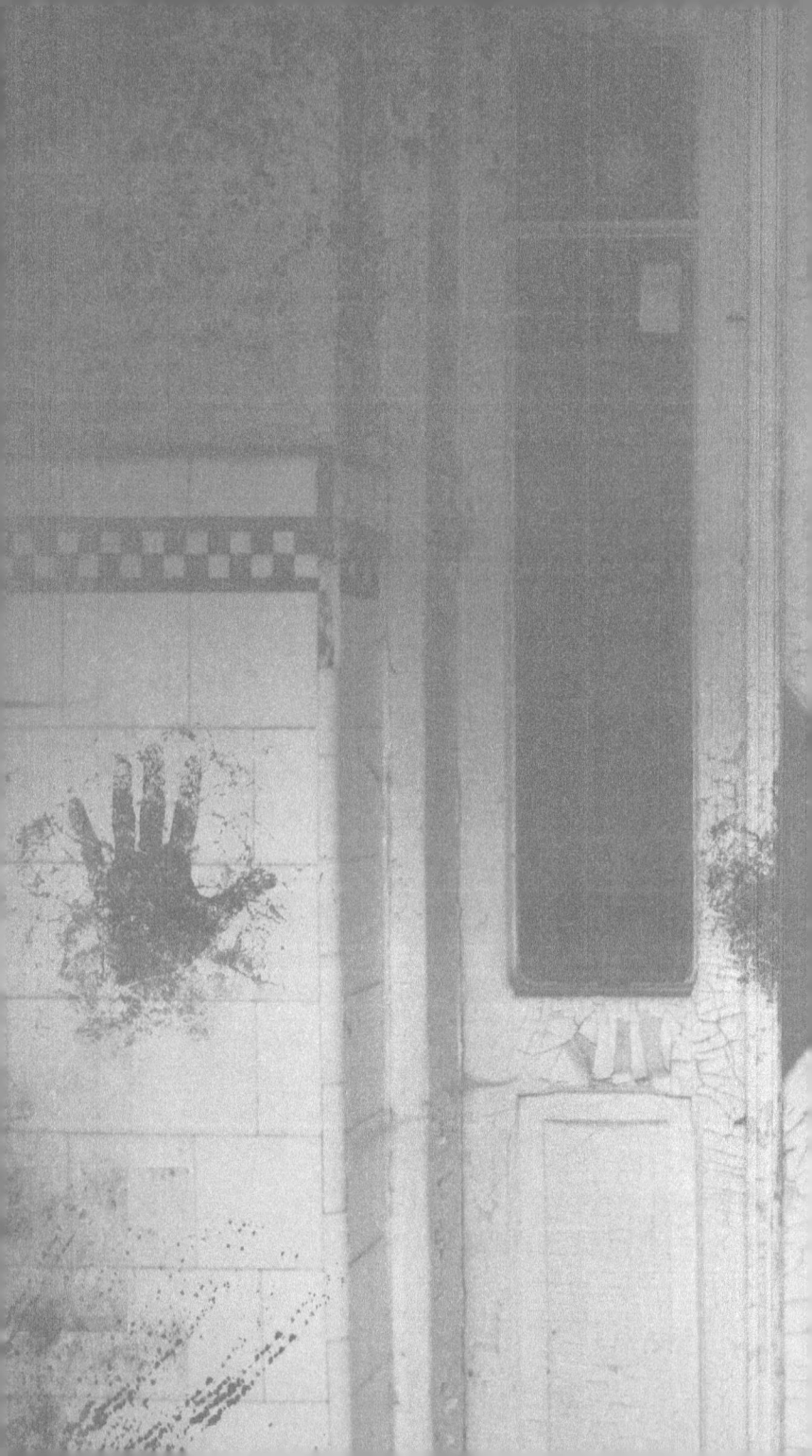

NOT EVERY STORY HAS A HAPPY ENDING...

Here, my friends, is a collection of my short stories. Each one has a name, literally, of a character contained within. I do hope you are ready for chills, scares, and possibly having to stop reading when something goes bump in the night.

I hope you enjoy.

JIMMY

Part 1

The sound of beeping began to penetrate Mike's dream. The noise was faint at first, like it was in the distance, but as it continued, it became louder. It was his dream after all; he could turn it off if he wanted to...

But there was another beep, this time louder than the last.

Before opening his eyes, he reached his hand over to where his alarm clock should be. He knew he could hit the snooze button three times before he had to actually open his eyes. As he moved his arm, he could only raise it four inches off the bed before something stopped him. He tried to pull his hand to him and again he met resistance.

Don't panic, he told himself.

He took several deep breaths as his eyes opened, adjusting to his surroundings. He looked down at his wrist. There was a canvas strap attached to a padded cuff around it. Glancing further down, he saw that it was attached to the rail.

What? His bed didn't have a rail.

A sharp pain shot though his stomach as he attempted to sit, almost panicking when he felt a stabbing pain on the right side of his head as he fell back into the pillow.

As he lay back down, his mom stood over him.

"Slowly, sweetie," she said with a smile, her voice sounding a bit hoarse. "You're still a little weak."

He looked into her eyes, realizing she had been crying. Her hair was pulled back into the ponytail she wore around the house when she was cleaning or relaxing. She never went out like that.

"Where am I?" He heard his own voice crack, his throat burning with each word.

"You're in the hospital," his mom said as she brought a straw to his parched lips. He took a sip. The cold water shocked his system, and he began to cough. He tried again to bring his hand to cover his mouth and failed.

"Hospital?" he heard himself ask between coughs, as if it was a complete question.

He saw his mother's face shift. It was so subtle, but he was familiar with her tells. She's worried. She looked at him, her lips parted as if she wanted to speak. But as quickly as her mouth opened, it closed again.

She offered him another sip from the straw. He took it, then she placed the cup down and took his hand. "Mike, baby, do you remember anything from the other night?" Her voice was almost a whisper as she looked down at his hand, refusing to meet his gaze.

He closed his eyes, trying to remember what led him here. He remembered school; he remembered coming home. It's just... a jumble of pictures.

Was I in a car? Was there an accident? Was I driving somewhere?

His stomach tightened with each question until he tried to jerk his hand away. His mom's hand just tightened around his, as if she thought that would somehow offer support as the memories came flooding back.

"I don't..." he began out loud, then his voice trailed off.

He had been sitting in his room, reading the page he'd just written in his journal.

He remembered the note he had written to his mom.

He opened his eyes and looked into his mother's hazel ones staring back at him, tears streaking down her face. He realized he had ones to match.

"I'm sorry," she said. "I am so sorry, Mikey. I am so, so sorry. I didn't understand. I didn't realize..."

He closed his eyes again, turning his head from hers as she tried to comfort him.

I remember now. He had taken the entire bottle of pills, the ones for his "depression," with a bottle of wine he had stolen from his parents.

He lay there on the bed, turned as far as the restraints would allow him, listening to the monitors, his mother's sobs, and her soft voice trying to comfort him, numb.

After several minutes, he heard a door open and looked up to see who had entered. He attempted to bring his hand up to his face again. It was his father, who looked as if he hadn't slept in days. Following him was a man in a lab coat Mike could only assume was a doctor.

"Mike, you're awake," his father said and smiled.

He attempted a weak smile back at his father, but all he could manage was a grimace as a wave of pain returned to his stomach.

After the spasm stopped, the doctor asked him, "How are you feeling?"

"Sore" was his only reply. How do I look like I am feeling? He thought as the doctor continued gazing at him.

The doctor smiled at him again and said, "You're a lucky kid. If your mom hadn't found you when she did, you might not be with us now."

As usual, Mike couldn't say what he was thinking; he wanted to scream that he didn't feel lucky at all, and he wished his mom hadn't found him, that the tears he cried were not due to being sad but were because he failed.

"Lucky, I guess" was all he said.

The doctor told him that he had been in the hospital for three days and that he had been in a coma because his heart had stopped. That Mike had, in fact, been dead for several minutes. Mike realized the last part the doctor had stated, not to explain the gravity of his health situation, but to scare him. It didn't. Mike assumed death was most likely less painful than what he was going through now.

As the doctor continued to speak, Mike heard less and less of what was being said. He nodded his head and said the obligatory "uh-huhs" when there were pauses and started to look around the room he was in. To his right, there was a small table with some cards, flowers, and balloons. There was even a teddy bear, no doubt from his family. He didn't have any friends.

He glanced to his left, nodding when he heard a questioning tone in the doctor's voice and realized there was a curtain pulled to the edge of his bed. His wasn't the only bed in the room. Just great.

Because the curtain was drawn, he couldn't see if it was occupied. As he turned his head back to the right to see if the doctor was almost finished, he had another sudden sharp pain on the right side of his head. Instinctively, he reached for the area, but the canvas straps still held him in place. Frustrated, he pushed his head back into the pillow.

His mom jumped to his side and began to say, "Mike, don't touch it. It needs to adjust..." but she was cut off by the doctor who said, "Michael, you fell and hit your head on the desk in your room. There was a nasty cut that required several stitches. If it is hurting, we can give you a little something for the pain."

"When can I get these off?" Mike said as he held up his hands to gesture to the restraints.

"Soon. We just need to ensure you won't try to hurt yourself again," the doctor replied. This created a slightly awkward silence.

Taking some cue, the doctor continued to speak with the same innocuous smile he had shown before. "Now that you're awake, we can begin your therapy sessions as soon as tomorrow if you would like, and we shall see from there. Sound good?"

"Great" was all Mike could say.

"We're going to let you get some rest now. We will talk some more soon," the doctor added as he injected something into the IV in Mike's arm.

Any thoughts of protesting were moot as he realized it must have been pain medication for his head. It made him instantly drowsy. As his eyes began to close, he heard indistinct talking. Something about an introduction happening, then the words became subdued. All Mike could think about was how great another therapist would be. He hated therapy, he thought, and fell into blackness.

PART 2

Mike couldn't tell how long he slept, but it must now be morning because the room seemed brighter from behind his closed lids than it was before. He listened to see if his parents were still in the room before opening his eyes. He heard the hums and beeps of the machines and nothing else. His eyes cracked open.

Out of habit, he tried to move his arm to push himself up, only to realize he was still restrained. With an exasperated sigh, he rolled onto his back and stared up at the ceiling.

"Feel like a dog on short leash?" he heard from his left.

The voice startled him. He turned his head slowly to his left, assuming the curtain was still in place. Instead, he saw that the curtain on the bed next to him had been drawn back, and he was looking at a boy about his age staring back at him. The boy raised his hand in a mock gesture of shaking hands to show he was similarly restrained. "My name is Jimmy, and you are?"

"Mike," he replied.

"They'll only keep you restrained for a few days. That is, unless you look like you are going to attempt again, then they may never take them off." Mike realized this caused his anger to rise before he noticed Jimmy was smirking at him. "I am just messing with you, Mike."

Mike didn't know what to say next. "So how did you fail to kill yourself?" didn't seem like a social thing to ask his roomie. Not that Mike was ever very good at the social stuff. Just ask all of the friends I don't have, he thought.

He opted for awkward silence instead and looked back up at the ceiling.

"Wondering how I tried to do it?" Jimmy asked after a couple minutes.

Yes, Mike thought as he considered his failed attempt to end his own life. He said nothing, like he always did, trying in some morbid way to be invisible.

"I jumped," Jimmy finally said after another long silence. "I supposed I should have picked a higher place, but of course, I thought I would be looking at it from the cheap seats now."

Mike smiled a little at that. He felt the exact same way when he remembered the look on his mom's face. If he hadn't failed, he would never have seen that.

When you're killing yourself, he supposed, you don't think you are going to fail and look back at yet another part of your life you didn't get to go your way. He hadn't.

He was about to open his mouth to make a comment when he heard their room door open. He turned to look at a nurse coming in with a wheelchair. He was about to ask what the chair was for when he saw it being parked next to Jimmy's bed.

As the nurse began to open up a cabinet on the other side of the room, she said, "It is time for your first therapy session, Michael." He sighed, but Jimmy just winked at him.

Mike took stock, for the first time, of his roommate. Jimmy was thin with light brown hair cut short, a light completion, and blue eyes. He wasn't the type of person most would pick out of a crowd except for one key feature, a scar that ran from his temple almost all the way to his chin on the right side of his face.

As Mike took a closer look, he also saw that Jimmy wasn't really moving his legs. They were bandaged in a couple of places, and there were red lines that showed they'd been recently healed.

Mike realized he was staring when Jimmy said, "Gnarly, huh?" He looked up and met Jimmy's eyes. He found Jimmy smiling at him, the scar almost invisible when he did. Mike found himself not looking away, and actually nodded and smiled back.

The curtain was suddenly drawn closed between his bed and Jimmy's. He had forgotten the nurse was there. She moved up the railing of the bed, undoing each restraint in turn.

"Put these on, sweetie," the nurse said as she gestured to a pile of fabric at the end of the bed. The nurse had also grabbed a blanket and placed it next to the clothes. She went back out the now drawn curtain and stated, "Just holler for me when you are ready." With that, he heard the door close.

He rubbed his wrists and sat up in the bed, swinging his legs over the side, making sure he still could. As he stood up, the first thing that hit him was that he was dizzy and very weak. So much so that he fell back onto the bed and had to breathe slowly through the renewed pain in his stomach and head. As he lay there, he heard a faint buzzing.

Do I really have to move? he thought. He knew the answer. The nurse, although apparently sweet in her demeanor, would be more than happy to "assist" him in getting ready for his session. He wasn't the least bit interested in being manhandled in his current condition.

He slowly sat up again, the buzzing and pain lessening as he took his time. He placed one foot then the other on the floor and, using the bed for support, worked his way down to grab the clothes. Then, using the wall to brace himself, he slowly made his way to the bathroom. He placed the clothes on a bench and carefully made his way to the sink, holding on with his right hand and turning on the facet with his left. He didn't want to leave his ability to stand to chance.

He looked at himself for the first time in days. What he saw looking back was terrible. The first thing he saw was that his hair had been cut very short. He was paler than normal, had large bags under his eyes, and the entire right side of his face was horrible bruised. He turned his head to get a closer look.

The bruising went from somewhere in his hairline to under his chin. A bandage covered what he assumed was his head wound behind his right ear. The doctor said he had fallen. He knew he wasn't supposed to, but he pulled away the bandage and looked at the two-inch cut. It had at least a dozen stitches. He couldn't help but wonder, as he looked at his injury, if the desk had survived any better.

He replaced the bandage, closed his eyes, and felt the familiar feeling of tears begin to well up in his eyes. His mother had found him. He wasn't going to let it happen—he wasn't going to cry. I won't let Jimmy hear that, he thought.

He took a deep breath in and slowly let it out. Then another.

The deep breaths helped him recover from the flood of self-pity with the realization that his breath was terrible. However many days of not brushing his teeth was nothing short of disgusting. He focused all his attention on the need to brush his teeth right then.

As he looked around, he saw only one toothbrush on the ledge. As he reached for it, he stopped. That one must have been Jimmy's. He opened the mirror to find a similar toothbrush as the one on the counter still in plastic wrap. He opened it up, brushed his teeth, and placed it back on the bottom shelf of the cabinet to keep it separate from Jimmy's. He had never shared a room with anyone before, but it seemed that sharing toothbrushes would be just as gross to his roommate as it was to him, even if by accident.

He dressed and slowly made his way out of the bathroom. The nurse was waiting for him with the wheelchair. He debated protesting, but as a wave of dizziness hit him, he realized he was in no position to do anything but accept her help. He sat down, and she wrapped the blanket around his legs.

"See you on the other side," he heard Jimmy say as he was wheeled out of the room.

PART 3

As he left the room for the first time he could remember, Mike was able to determine that he must be on the ground floor of the hospital or close to it. He could see trees out of the small rectangular window at the end of the hall.

The nurse did not stop talking the entire time she wheeled him through the small maze of corridors. As they made a final turn to the right, he knew that he was in a series of offices instead of normal hospital rooms. Mike also knew that he would not find his way back to the room without help. All the offices looked the same, and he assumed they were all for therapy.

The nurse opened a door with a press of a button and wheeled him in. A couch and two chairs with a small coffee table in between were the only furniture in the room. The nurse, whose name was Carla he had found out on their brief journey, offered to help him onto the couch.

Realizing he still didn't feel right, Mike took the assistance and said, "Thank you" once he was seated on the couch.

Carla smiled, said, "You're welcome. See you in a bit," and left the room.

He was looking around at the walls when the door opened, and the doctor from earlier walked in carrying a small tray with containers on it.

"I thought you might be hungry," the doctor stated with a smile as he nodded toward the food. He put the tray on the table so that it was within Mike's reach.

The doctor reached out his hand to shake and said, "Michael, my name is Dr. Epeton. How are you feeling today?"

"Fine and it is Mike," he replied, shaking the doctor's hand.

"Mike, I know you don't like therapy. Your parents told me that you didn't think it helped," the doctor said as he seated himself. As the doctor continued to talk, Mike opened the containers to find applesauce, a broth of some kind, and finally some chocolate pudding. He took the pudding and a plastic spoon lying on the napkin on the tray. He noticed that was the only silverware available.

"You have been through a lot, and the last thing you want is some doctor telling you how you should feel and that it will all be better. I am not going to do that. I am just going to ensure that you are not going to attempt to take your life again. When

I am pretty sure that is the case, then I will release you. If we work together, we can make that happen fast." There was a pause in the talking then, and Mike realized the doctor was waiting for a response.

"Great" was all he decided he should say.

Dr. Epeton smiled again and asked, "So how about I ask you a bunch of questions, and we talk a bit and see where it goes from there?"

Mike nodded, scooping pudding into his mouth.

He was with Dr. E, as the doc wanted him to call him, for about two hours. He knew how to do the song and dance. He opened up just a little. He didn't want the doctor to think it was easy and explained how hard life was as a teenager in world that didn't understand him. It was painfully predictable, and so was the diagnosis. He was "depressed."

As usual, the doctor was able to tell him that "there is hope" and "it actually could get better for you," but only if he was "willing to try." It took everything for Mike not to roll his eyes. He had heard it before, almost word for word, and as with all therapy, it never changed.

When the session was complete, Carla came back, helped him into the wheelchair, and took him back to his room.

PART 4

"You survived," Jimmy said with a small laugh.

Mike shrugged.

"I know. My doctor told me I wasn't crazy. That was a first. Not really. They all say that, don't they?" Jimmy laughed as he grabbed something off the side table. "Hey, I scored us a remote. Wanna watch something?"

Mike did, so he moved so he could see the TV. Being cuffed, it was a bit uncomfortable. They watched movies for a couple hours. When they got bored with the movies, they began to play a game of truth. Telling each other personal information in turn, they talked about school, parents, and girls. He found out that Jimmy played most of the same video games he did, and that he had pretty much the same hobbies. Jimmy's favorite movie was Aliens, which was one of Mike's favorites as well.

It was dark out when the nurse came in again to give him some of the pain medication that put him right to sleep, the sound of TV in the background.

When lunch was brought in the next day, it interrupted their movie, mainly because the nurse insisted the TV be shut off for mealtime. He was finishing more pudding when his parents walked in. His mom began to smile as she walked up to give him a hug.

"You look good," she said as she squeezed him a little tightly.

"Thanks," he replied.

Mike was about to introduce his parents to Jimmy when he looked over to see that Jimmy had fallen asleep. His mother walked over in the direction he was looking.

"So, this must be Jimmy? Are you going to introduce us to your new friend?" she asked, using her "hostess" voice as she turned back to him.

"He's sleeping," Mike said quietly, looking at his mom a bit confused.

"Oh, well," his mother quietly said as she pulled the curtain between the beds closed, "why don't you tell us all about him then?"

He told his parents about his new "roomie." When he finished saying only what he thought he had to, his mother said,

"Well, I look forward to meeting him." And she smiled again in the direction of the closed curtain.

"How did you know his name?" Mike finally asked, realizing he had not brought up Jimmy to his parents.

"Well, you see…" His mom started to hesitantly explain before his father jumped in with, "Dr. E. told us you made a friend, so we wanted to find out more about him." His mother nodded with each word.

So, Dr. E. was spying on him—just great. Well maybe making a new friend would convince the great doctor to let him out sooner.

His dad set a bag on his lap. They brought him some clothes, a couple of comic books, and his handheld gaming system so that he could play a little.

As he looked through the bag, Mike noticed there were a few of his favorite snacks as well. His mom always gave him snacks when she felt guilty. He looked up and thanked his parents.

"How long do I have to stay here?" Mike finally decided to ask.

His dad told him that the doctor didn't think it would take that long, and he should be able to go home soon. He could tell that this news made his parents happy.

They visited for about two hours, telling him all about the happenings with his family and neighbors. He listened and nodded like he always did when his mom tried to include him, as if he were involved or interested at all.

It wasn't long after his parents left that Jimmy woke up. When he asked what he missed, Mike told him about his parents visiting and the stuff his parents had dropped off.

Mike shared everything with Jimmy. Taking turns, they challenged each other on the videogame and spend hours swapping stories. They also ate all the snacks by the next day. This did not help the pain in Mike's stomach, but it did cheer him up a little.

PART 5

The days began to roll by. The therapy was mandatory. Sometimes two to three times a day, he met with Dr. E. Some days seemed to be better than others, and of course, it was always better when he was medicated.

The doctor had put him on a medicine for his depression, and when he wasn't making any progress, the nurses realized he hadn't been swallowing his pills and resorted to administering the medication via the IV.

The new drugs made him tired. They always had some sort of side effect; the last ones had made him nauseous all the time. He supposed it didn't matter what they did to him as long as they made him happy, even if he was sleeping through half of his life.

He listened to Dr. E. speak, hearing the noise of the doctor's voice, but not the words. Sometimes he did that—just faded out and only heard the noise of people speaking around him. He found that he did this a lot, with teachers, his parents, and the kids he disliked at school. He suddenly heard himself ask, "Are you treating Jimmy?"

Dr. E. looked at him, stunned for a moment. "I can't talk about other patients. You know that." The doctor gave him a fake smile, the kind a person gives when he wants to drop the subject. His mother did that a lot.

"I wasn't asking you to talk about other patients; I was asking if he was in therapy with you," he persisted.

"Why do you want to know that?" the doctor asked.

"He never has visitors," Mike said, meeting the doctors' gaze perfectly. Dr. E. had a look flash across his face for only a second, but there was something there.

"His dad visits him. He visits him in his physical therapy sessions," the doctor said as he closed his notepad. "We can pick this up again tomorrow. You look tired." He pushed the button at the door that called for the nurse.

When he got back to his bed, he found Jimmy playing on the game system. "So, how is our friend Mike doing today? Is he cured?" Jimmy said without looking up from the unmistakable sounds of the Mario Brothers game.

"Yep, all good. Should be out of here by the morning," he responded.

He looked up at the ceiling tiles and blew his bangs out of his vision. His hair had grown out. He wouldn't let them cut it. In some weird way, it measured his incarceration time in inches. His fingers brushed along the scar. The bump to his head had healed finally. There was a small hard knot that felt flat with little bumps. The doctor had told him it was scar tissue from when they had gone back in to fix something wrong with the way it was healing. It hurt a little when he rubbed it.

As he found himself following the lattice work of ceiling tiles, he asked, "Does your dad visit you?" He heard the sound of the game music stop suddenly.

"What?" Jimmy asked, sounding a bit surprised.

"I never see them, your parents. I was just wondering if you saw them." There was pause. Looking over, he saw Jimmy staring at him with an unhappy look on his face.

"Sorry, dude. I didn't mean…" He began to say, but Jimmy cut him off.

"It's fine. My dad works a lot so I see him when he can, just not as much as… well… not a lot." Jimmy turned back to his game, and the sounds started up again.

The nurse came in then for his next dose, and within a few moments, Mike let himself go to into the abyss of sleep. It was a convenient way to let the subject drop.

PART 6

When he woke up hours later, Jimmy was not in his bed, and Mike's head was hurting again. He must have rubbed it too hard earlier. As he reached to touch the area where the pain was coming from, he found another bandage. He called the nurse to let him off his leash to use the restroom.

When he got up, he was a little dizzy, and his mouth was really dry. He slowly stood and made his way to the restroom where he turned on the water and looked into the mirror. He lifted the bandage to another set of stitches. What had happened?

When he finished, he washed his hands and noticed the toothbrush on the counter was in the same exact place as the first day he had seen it. He held it up, and it was dry. This meant nothing until he pulled his own from the cabinet and held them side by side. Jimmy's hadn't been used. He put them both back and made his way back to the bed.

He asked the nurse, "What happened to my head?" All she would say was that the doctor would explain. He asked her to get him some juice or something cold to drink. As she re-attached his restraints, she promised she would.

He closed his eyes. It had been months, and he was no closer to getting out of here than the first day he woke up. He had been saying all the right things to the great Dr. E. and yet he was lying in the same bed, restrained, and nothing had changed.

He heard the door open and shut again just as he was about to go into another wave of self-pity.

"Whatcha doing?" Jimmy asked, startling him for a moment. Jimmy, it seemed, was a ninja. He had an ability to be completely silent, then just appear. Jimmy said it was because he had been invisible to most people all his life that he must have adopted it as a superpower. Mike knew exactly how that felt.

"I would say wallowing in self-pity, but that doesn't sound nearly as cool as thinking about hot sexy cheerleaders," Mike chimed back.

"I like cheerleaders, especially the really bitchy ones. They are the hottest of them all," Jimmy retorted as he propped himself on his side.

"What's with you?" he asked Jimmy.

"Well, besides the newfound joy of never-ending sponge baths, I won't walk again. Doctor said the nerve damage will make it so it is impossible, even with physical therapy," Jimmy said as if he was still talking about bitchy cheerleaders.

Mike didn't know what to say, so he stayed silent as he always did.

"You don't have to say anything. I figured it out before they told me, and nothing was changing with the physical therapy, so it was sort of a given. Didn't mean to make it weird. Sorry, bro." Jimmy winked at him, then smiled.

Mike realized that Jimmy was the only friend he had since grade school. He didn't always know how to act or what to say, but Jimmy did. It threw him off sometimes, but at other times, he felt relief.

They watched some action/comedy movie with Bruce Willis for the next couple of hours; the end scene was some guy being thrown off a building followed by some brilliant comedic tagline that was terribly overused. As Jimmy began looking for the remote, Mike looked over and asked, "Do you ever think about doing it again? Jumping, I mean."

"Yes, well, I think about how I would do it. I mean, I can't really jump again," Jimmy said, gesturing down to his legs.

"I think I would have to be surer next time that it would really be done. I mean, I can't wake up after my mom finds me. That can't happen again," he said, feeling more emotion than he thought. "Although, I don't see how it will happen if I can't get out of here." He slammed his hand down and felt the restraint on his arm slide up and down.

"Why would it have to be after?" Jimmy asked, but before he could reply, he heard the door open. Dr. E. walked in.

"Good, you're awake. How are you feeling?" Dr. E. asked.

"Why do I have more stitches?" he asked back, sounding more aggressive than he intended.

"We found something in the scar tissue, the way it had healed, and we had to make an adjustment. This should be the last." Dr. E. smiled the same way he did at each therapy session.

"When can I get these off?" Mike said gesturing to the restraints and ignoring the fact his previous question went unanswered.

"Actually, that is part of what I am here for. You can have them off today. I just need you to understand that doesn't give you permission to roam the halls. But this way you can move around your room comfortably. How does that sound?" Dr. E. sounded like a ride host at Disney when he wanted to with his perfectly calm voice.

"Great." Mike faked a big smile to seal the deal.

He looked over at Jimmy, who gave him a little nod for his performance. Dr. E. bought it fully because he smiled back and said, "I am glad to see you doing so well, Mike." As he was turning to leave, Dr. E. patted him on the shoulder in acknowledgement or comfort, Mike wasn't sure which. He was just glad when the doc was gone.

Part 7

It wasn't until later in the evening that the nurse came in to remove the restraints. There was a long list of do's and don'ts he had to sign and initial. When it was finally over, he sat up in bed for the first time, stretching his arms above his head.

"Free at least, free at last," he heard Jimmy chanting beside him.

He looked over and realized that his happiness was slightly short lived; Jimmy was still restrained. He got up and went to the side of Jimmy's bed. He didn't want to leave his friend bound, but when he grabbed the restraints, he saw they were secured with a lock and key. He sat back on his bed.

"Don't worry about it, dude. Mine will be off soon. Always happens that way," Jimmy assured him.

"How would you know that?" he asked back, not looking up from his own freed wrists.

"Honestly, well, this is not my first time as a 'guest' of this hospital. This is actually my third round locked away in this tower." Jimmy's voice sounded almost proud.

"What?" Mike said in a whisper. He was stunned.

"They say third time is a charm, right?" Jimmy was smiling, but the smile didn't reach his eyes.

Mike just sat there. He didn't know what to say. He couldn't imagine putting his parents through that kind of pain, over and over, especially after seeing his parents' faces the first morning he woke up. He would rather see them grieve and be able to move on than put them through that again.

"I didn't think I would get caught. That is why. The last time was a sure thing," Jimmy replied to the unspoken question.

When he met Jimmy's gaze, Mike could see it then, the disappointment of being here, of being in that bed.

"Is that why I never see your family visit?" Mike asked as he continued to make eye contact. Normally, he would look away.

He wanted to, but on some level, he had no choice.

Jimmy broke the link by looking down, biting his lip for a moment as if he were nervous. "My dad can see me anytime he wants. He works here."

Ten questions immediately raced through Mike's mind. Before he could ask one of them, Jimmy said, "Yes, he works here. Yes, you have seen him. You know him, in fact." Mike was confused, and he was sure it was showing on his face. He tried to remember all the males he had met during his stay, and before he could even guess, Jimmy stunned him again.

"Dr. E. is my dad, Mike," Jimmy stated flatly.

Mike lay back on his bed, his head swimming, and knew this feeling. When things were about to get really bad for him, this is how he felt just before. He felt a sharp pain in his head where the scar was.

"I am sorry. Dude, I am really sorry I didn't tell you before. My father made me promise. He said that it would affect his ability to help you if you knew he couldn't help his own son," Jimmy said as he sighed. "Well, maybe not the last part. He thought I was better, you know, but then again, father or no, they always think you're better until you jump off the hospital roof four stories up."

Jimmy stated it so matter-of-factly.

"How did you get up there? All the doors are locked." It came out of his mouth before he could even think.

"I got a key from one of the janitors. I told him I wanted to put something in my Dad's office to surprise him for his birthday. It was a lot easier than you would think." Jimmy had that proud look again.

"Four floors, huh? You survived that?" he asked. He was calming down, his head now more of a dull ache.

Just before Jimmy was able to answer, the door opened, and Dr. E. and the nurse stepped in the room, both a bit winded.

An awkward silence followed. Unsure of whom the doctor was eager to speak with, both of them just sat there looking at Dr. E.

The doctor cleared his throat and said, "Michael, are you okay?" The doctor had resorted to using his full name again, and that was never good.

"Great," he said flatly.

The doctor walked up to him and pulled out one of those flashlights, shining it in each eye while holding up his eyelids. He then pulled an otoscope out of his pocket and looked in Mike's right ear. When the doctor seemed satisfied with whatever he was looking for, he put both devices back in his pocket.

"You are sure you're fine?" Dr. E asked again. "No pain, dizziness, nausea?"

Although he had all of those moments ago, Mike knew that if the doctor were asking like this, it usually meant something was wrong, and it would mean tests or medication at the very least. He was not interested in either.

"Nope, all good." He nodded his head as if this would confirm his words.

"Okay, then. If anything changes, please let the nurse know." Mike used another series of nods until the doctor and nurse left.

As the door closed, he turned back to Jimmy. "He didn't even look at you. What was that about?"

Jimmy shrugged. "I didn't exist much to him before. I guess it doesn't surprise me now."

Jimmy flipped the TV on and lay back in bed. Mike guessed he was done talking about it. Jimmy didn't really speak the rest of the night. Mike fell asleep to the sounds of explosions and snappy dialogue, which had to be a Michael Bay movie.

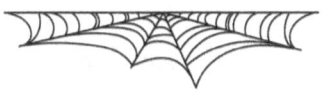

Part 8

He woke up to hear half of a muffled conversation. It sounded like his mother's voice. "Was he hurt? Well, how do you know that? I don't think this is a good idea anymore. I want..." The hushed speaking was cut off when Mike rolled over in bed.

"What is not a good idea anymore?" he asked, looking at his mother. She was worried. He could always tell, and she looked from him to Dr. E. as if waiting for approval to respond.

Dr. E. finally took the lead after an awkward silence. "We were just discussing the next phase of treatment." As he finished, Mike's mom looked down to her hands. That wasn't it, he thought. His Mom always looked down when something wasn't completely true.

"So, what is the next phase, doc?" he asked, the tension getting thicker.

"Well, Michael, I think the best thing for you right now would be to stay here until we have your medication at the correct level, and we have a chance to ensure you are in a good place," Dr. E. answered.

He looked at his mom again. There were tears in her eyes. She wouldn't meet his look. He looked up at his father, whose hand was resting on her shoulder. His lips were pursed. His father held his gaze for only a moment, then he too looked away.

"Great." He rolled over to face away from the crowd. He saw his mother's hand reach out as he moved but never felt it touch him.

Moments later, he heard the door close. That was it. He was alone. He was always alone, and there was always something wrong with him.

Part 9

"You up?" he asked Jimmy after a few minutes of lying in silence, listening to the machines beep.

"Yup," he heard in reply.

"Tell me how you did it again," he said flatly. Jimmy rolled over and looked at him for a moment. He wasn't sure if Jimmy was going to give him some speech about how he shouldn't even consider what he was thinking. He felt the swirl of emotions start to take hold. As if sensing Mike was near his breaking point, Jimmy began to tell him the story in complete detail. Every time a question popped into his head, it was answered by Jimmy before he could ask it.

What Jimmy explained was perilous at times. The plan relied on not getting caught by anyone because that would result in the restraints going back on. The one thing he knew was that he wasn't staying until the great doctor thought he was in a "good place."

He was about to ask the final question that came to mind when Jimmy said, "I can't" and pulled up on his restraints. Mike nodded. When he thought about it, he knew that the route he would have to take would involve stairs, which Jimmy wasn't equipped to handle either.

He waited until the nurse checked on him at 11:00pm. As the nurse was putting the final dosage for the day in his IV, she said, "Sweet dreams." He nodded and rolled over as if the medicine was taking effect. A few moments later, the light was turned out. He sat up in bed, listening to the sound of retreating footsteps.

He got out of the bed, letting go of the IV line which began to empty liquid onto the sheets. He bunched up his clothes and an extra blanket to make it look like he was sleeping, then pulled the blanket over the top.

He crept up to the door for one last check to see that all was as Jimmy described. As he turned back, Jimmy was smiling at him.

"Thanks, man, for everything." It was all he could think of to say to the only true friend he ever had.

Jimmy nodded his head and said, "Good luck, dude." He matched each of Jimmy's steps perfectly, and everything was exactly as he had stated. Winding through the corridors, he finally found the janitor closet Jimmy described, and as he glanced to his left, he found the key hook right where he was told it would be. He took a set of keys and continued to make his way.

As he neared the stairwell, he looked around and saw that he was not near the actual hospital rooms anymore. These were offices. He looked at the nametags and found the second one on the right had Dr. Epeton—Neuroscience. He looked down at the keys and decided he had to try. On the fourth key, he heard the click of the lock, and the door slid open.

He quietly entered and shut the door behind him. Taking a deep breath, he walked over to the desk which faced away from the wall that held a huge picture window. The window allowed for a great view of the hospital grounds and, in turn, light to flood in from the well-lit hospital grounds.

He sat in the great doctor's chair. While debating if he should leave a note, which did not go so well the last time, he noticed a family picture. It looked like it was taken at one of the family theme parks because it had the park logo. Mike picked it up and held it in the light. It was the doctor, his wife, and Jimmy, and said May 4th 2002. He moved the picture to another angle and looked at the date again.

He placed the photo back on the desk, puzzled. Pulling open the drawers, he found the file with his name on it and began to read it. It was all medical terms, mostly medications and dosages. There were references to the surgeries he had, including the most recent one for his head trauma, implant adjustments, predicable software modifications... He continued reading what looked like version updates when he heard someone whisper, "What are you doing?" He jumped in his seat, his heart racing. He looked up to see Jimmy sitting across the desk from him.

"I was..." Mike started to say when Jimmy said, "I didn't hear any alarms, so I wasn't sure if you got caught or changed your mind."

"No," he said, shaking his head. "I wanted... Wait, how did you get up here? Is this you?" he asked, pointing at the picture on the desk.

Jimmy reached out, grabbed the picture, and nodded his head. "Yup, last spring, family bonding trip." He placed the picture back on the desk.

"Better get going," Jimmy said. "You only have about five more minutes, and they will be in to check on you." Mike looked down at the phone to see the time; it was 12:04am on 09-04-2010. Nodding back, he looked up at Jimmy, then grabbed the picture and headed to the door to the stairwell.

As Mike grabbed the door handle, he glanced back one last time at his friend sitting in the wheelchair in front of his father's desk. Jimmy looked exactly the same as the photo in Mike's hand from 2002. Jimmy hadn't aged a day.

Looking back down at the photo, Mike guessed why Dr. E. had chosen the Jimmy from eight years ago and wondered for a moment when the last time the good doctor had seen his Jimmy. He took one last deep breath and headed up the stairs.

He knew that when he opened the roof door, the alarm would sound, and he would have two minutes. Mike pushed the door open, and in less than a second, the alarm triggered.

It was louder than he expected. In the next moment, the emergency roof lights switched on. Two minutes, he thought, and he began moving again, items in hand.

It only took twenty seconds, thanks to Jimmy.

CHARLIE

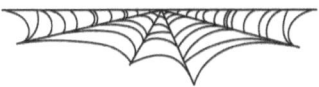

The alarm sounded when Savannah became aware of the door opening.

Security in that portion of the building was tremendous. To start, one had to navigate a labyrinth of bio-driven security panels, then a slow entry through several pressurized doors that make a sucking sound when the seals popped.

Savannah knew the confined ventilation in her building was designed to protect employees from possible leaks contaminating the "non-secure sections" of the facility. That made her smile a little. She had thought on several occasions how silly it was that the people working with the dangerous chemicals were not protected from their own mistakes.

She lay on her side, her back against the wall farthest from the door. She had originally tried to sit up, but as she grew weaker, she slid down from her original position, unable to maintain the strength to hold herself up.

The floor felt cold against her skin, so cold it almost burned. She stared at the flower lying before her, the light reflecting from its glass petals. As her vision blurred, it looked almost like a kaleidoscope.

Remembering the door, she slowly tilted her head up, catching a glimpse of her visitor. Her eyes had a hard time focusing, and she could only see a shadowy figure in the doorway. She let her head drop down again; it was too much to keep holding it up. It didn't matter who it was, it was too late for any of them. She had made sure of it.

"Van?" said a familiar voice.

She hoped that she had imagined it. Out of habit, she took a deep breath, hoping to steady her nerves. She knew she was almost done. Instead of calming her, the breath caused her to begin coughing and gagging. When she couldn't catch her breath, she began to panic. She felt hands grip her shoulders and prop her up to a sitting position.

Her eyes closed, she focused, then took a smaller breath, not too deep; she did it again and calmed herself. She knew she could do it. She had to.

The hands holding her shoulders attempted to pull her into an embrace, but she held her hand out and wheezed, "Stop."

The arms didn't stop, not until she was in a full embrace. She mustered enough strength to raise her head and looked into familiar caramel-colored eyes looking back at her from the mask of a biohazard suit.

His eyes were home to her. They were safe and warm and at that very moment portrayed a franticness she had never seen; one she had never hoped to see.

"Charlie... Please..." Her voice was a harsh whisper, unrecognizable even to her.

Charlie was speechless as he looked down at her, as if he couldn't comprehend what he was seeing. Savannah knew how she must look now if the experiments had been any indication of the results. The whites of her eyes would be a sickening orange color, including her lips, gums, and nasal passages. Her skin would appear ashen and almost scaly. That always happened before it began to fall off in little chunks. She wasn't sure if that had happened yet, but she knew it would.

She closed her eyes, unable to look at his distraught visage any longer. "Charlie... You shouldn't be here; you must go before..." Her voice erupted into another coughing fit .

He held on to her a little tighter to comfort her. Then he began to move, and she felt relief. He wasn't always the best at doing what she asked, but in this case, he has to, she thought.

As quickly as the relief came, it passed as she heard the crinkling of the suit and realized that he was adjusting to get a better hold on her and lift her up into his arms. With all her mustered strength, she pushed herself out of his grasp and fell to the floor.

When he reached for her again, she held her hand up and yelled, "No!"

Her eyes closed again. Focus on your breath, she thought as she felt another coughing fit coming on. "Please..." Her voice was barely a whisper. "Please, Charlie... Go." With a slow breath in and out, she continued, "Even if you... It's too late... I will die ... soon."

"But Van..." he began. She looked up at him through the protection that would save his life. There were tears streaming down his face.

"Please..." she said, lifting her hand toward his face, wanting to wipe the tears away before they fell. Her fingertips touched the plastic of the suit hood and slid off as she began coughing again uncontrollably. She felt her entire body begin to spasm, then just as suddenly stop.

Unable to draw another breath, she again felt the cool burn of the tiles against her face.

Then ... blackness.

Two Years Earlier

Fountains lined both sides of the cement walkway leading to the glass doors with the WVL logo in large, frosted letters. Savannah thought, *This will the best year of my life.*

Savannah, a graduate student from University of New Mexico, had dual master's degrees in biology and chemistry. Always at the top of her class, even with all her academic achievements and knowing she was in the top list of candidates for the program, she was still thrilled when she received the notification of her acceptance to the World Vision Laboratories fall internship program.

WVL headquarters was just outside of Boston, MA. Although she had travelled in her life, Savannah had never lived this far from her family. She had been nervous and excited for the months leading up to this moment. Renting a small studio apartment just a little over a mile from her work on the 128 loop that ran around Boston, she knew the internship would require many late nights, and she didn't want to risk traveling too far on the little sleep she was predicting she'd be getting.

She looked up to the mostly cloudless blue sky and thought there couldn't be a better day. Of course, just then she was bumped from behind and felt the chill of cold liquid going down her shoulder.

"Oh my god, I am so sorry," she heard from behind her as her arm involuntarily trembled from the chill.

She turned to look at her assailant.

He stood just several inches taller than her 5'10". With sandy brown hair cut short and looking as if he had just rolled out of bed, he had caramel brown eyes framed by black, horn-rimmed glasses and a cute dimple on his left cheek.

He began spouting, "I am such a klutz. I know it. I am sorry. My name is Charlie, and this is my first day, and I guess I'm nervous, and I wasn't paying attention. I'll pay for it, your shirt, to get cleaned. Oh god, I am so, so sorry."

Savannah finally raised her hand, stopping the flood of words coming from the very embarrassed... He said his name— Charlie. That was it.

Charlie stopped speaking at the introduction of her hand. She lowered it, took a breath, smiled, and said, "It's okay, really. Accidents happen."

He smiled at her again and said, "Thanks. My name is..."

"Charlie," she finished for him. "Yes, I remember from the apology. I'm Savannah." She reached out her hand.

Shifting the white Styrofoam cup into his other hand, he reached out to shake and began to speak again. "Nice to meet you, Savannah. I hope to run into you again sometime." He released her hand as the last words slipped from his lips, and he grimaced. "Bad choice of words. Well, this has been weird. I am going to go... because as much as I hate to say it, this can get much worse." With that, he smiled and gave a quick wave before he headed off toward the front doors.

Savannah assessed the damage to her clothes. Luckily, the iced coffee was only on her shoulder and the back part of her sleeve. She pulled a cardigan out of her bag, put it on, and headed for her future.

When she reached the front desk, she still marveled at actually being in WVL. The security guard behind the desk took her ID, and after several moments and a quick picture, he handed her a lanyard with an employee badge that had her name on it. When she placed it around her neck, she was beaming. It said INTERN in green letters at the bottom, but it meant it was official and she was a part of the team that led the way in bio-technological advances.

The security guard then handed her a packet with a small map. He pointed out a room marked with a small star where she needed to report for orientation.

She smiled. "Thank you," she said as she ascended the small flight of stairs.

She found the room easily enough. It had a placard on front of the double doors that said:

WELCOME INTERNS—TOGETHER WE
WILL CHANGE THE FUTURE

Savannah knew that this was her chance to do just that, change the future, for her and, she hoped, many countless others.

Savannah was on cloud nine when she walked through the doors into what looked like a slightly larger than normal conference room. An oval table that spanned the length of the room had futuristic looking clear plastic chairs pushed up to each place. On the table before each chair was a nametag with a symbol, a chilled bottle of water on a silver coaster, and a silver pen.

Out of habit, she counted the number of tags and found that there were 32. This surprised her because all the information she had gathered to this point told her that WVL only accepted two interns each year and usually only one in every twelve interns was eventually awarded a full-time position with the company.

She found her chair midway down the table and pulled it out so she could sit. She took out a notebook and reached for the pen just before her name tag. It felt heavy in her hand, and she saw that it was engraved: "What Is Your Future?" She turned the pen over in her hands as she heard other voices, and several more people came into the room.

She looked around the room as people arrived and found their places. The only decorations in the room were a series of oil paintings depicting a vineyard. As she continued to scan the room, her gaze fell on Charlie; he was seated near the head of the table. She realized she might have been staring when he met her gaze, smiled, and waved.

She waved back then looked down quickly. She didn't want to have another awkward encounter for the day and pretended to ready herself for the meeting when a hush fell over the room. Looking around to see what had caused that quiet, she was suddenly in awe. Standing at the head of the table was Dr. Leadly M. Sidelinger.

Dr. Sidelinger was the head of Research and Development at WVL. He was known as one, if not the brightest, mind in the field of biochemistry. Savannah had followed his work, and it was what had inspired her to go into that field of study.

Calm down, she thought. She took a deep breath, then closed her eyes. Savannah had mentally prepared herself for today. She was very confident in clinical situations and, when prepared, social ones, and when she applied for this internship, she had hoped, after achieving the position, she may one day meet him. She had no idea that day would be today.

"Welcome to World Vision Laboratories Fall Internship program," he began, then paused as there was a loud round of applause. "I am Dr. Sidelinger." Another round of applause, but this time he held up his hand to quiet the group.

"I know that many of you may be looking around and wondering why you are seated with 31 other interns." There were several nodding heads as he continued, "This year I decided to try a different methodology in finding our star candidates." He waited a beat, then said, "This year's internship program will progress differently than it has in the past. You will be divided up into teams. Each team will have four people for a total of eight teams. In each stage of the program, one person will be asked to step down from the internship group. When the groups are reduced to only two, they will be re-teamed to a group of four again. This process will continue until there is a solitary team of four. From this final group, two candidates will be chosen to join the team at World Vision Laboratories." Dr. Sidelinger took a moment to let this sink in for the room.

"Each stage of the program should take six months, and in three years, you will know if you have earned your position." There were some murmurs, but they were silenced when he concluded by saying, "I understand if this is more than you bargained for when you arrived here. Mr. Handleson will go over all the details that have been provided in your orientation packet, including compensation. Thank you all." With a final round of applause, he exited the room.

The gentleman who took the doctor's place at the head of the table was dressed in a WVL polo and khakis. "Hello. I am Mr. Josh Handleson. I am the head of the internship program this year. If you would, please open up the folders you were given at the start of the day. I will give you some time to review and sign the forms. I will be directly outside this room with your mentors for this program. Once you locate your mentor and all your team members have completed their forms, you will begin your first day of orientation." With that, he left the room.

Savannah reviewed and signed her forms, then headed out the door to find her mentor. She found him right away as he was holding up a sign with four names listed on it. He was quite tall, standing at about 6'5" with dark black hair, cut short. As she approached, he greeted her, "You must be Savannah Curtis." He reached out his hand. "I am Marcus Huntinger, and I will be your mentor for at least the first stage on the internship."

As she reached out her hand to shake his, she met his deep blue eyes and his very playful smirk. "Yes, it is nice to meet you," she said, sounding more surprised and confused than she intended.

"Don't worry. I make it a point to know the candidates I will be working with. You're prettier than your graduation photos," he said without a hint of sarcasm, and the smirk never leaving his face.

She was thankful that at that moment the other members of her team walked up and introduced themselves. There was Michelle Travis, a petite girl with wavy dark hair and tanned skin that Savannah guessed was of Latin heritage. Maliek Davis was a tall African American. He his hair was close shaven, and he had a bright smile. Last was Artemus Doukas, who was of Greek decent with olive skin and curly dark hair that fell just past his ears. Artemus was painfully shy in greeting his team, and Savannah could tell that he had a severe acne condition in his teenage years. He was shorter than she was, standing at about 5'7" and was slightly overweight.

That first day, Marcus started with a detailed tour of the facility. There had been a map included with the welcome packet, and he encouraged everyone on the team to take it out and mark a few key places. They learned that in addition to the floors topside, there were three underground levels as well. The bottom most level was restricted access, and Marcus would not discuss any aspect of what happened there.

When the tour ended, he showed everyone to the cafeteria for lunch. Savannah decided to sit outside at one of the tables that overlooked the manicured lawns and tree line that surrounded the property. It had warmed up, so she took off her sweater and placed it on the back of her chair. She had made a simple lunch of a peanut butter sandwich with cherry jam, a bottle of water, and an apple. While she ate, she ran over everything she had learned. She was finishing the last bite of her apple when she heard a voice behind her say, "What happened to your shirt?" It was Marcus.

She had forgotten about her morning encounter and the condition of her sleeve. She smiled and said, "A inconcinnus hominis."

Marcus squinted at her, then said, "A clumsy man, huh?" Savannah was stunned. She had no reason to use Latin to explain what had happened and wasn't even quite sure why she had, but Marcus had known exactly what she had said.

"Well, Savannah Curtis, I'm impressed with your vernacular, and you do look better as a ginger than a blonde." He smirked. He tilted his head toward the door. "See you in five." With that, he disappeared inside. A little flustered, she threw her trash away, quickly put her sweater back on, and headed toward her group.

On the first basement level, there was a communal locker room shared by the interns. Everyone already had a locker already assigned and found inside a lab coat in his or her correct size, all with the WVL logo. After they suited up, Marcus showed them to the lab. Once all security measures were discussed, Marcus passed out tablets to each member of the team. There was a 55- inch monitor on one wall, and as Marcus hit certain buttons on his tablet, it brought up information on the screen.

Savannah looked down on her tablet, and it had a square green box with a fingerprint symbol. She placed her finger on it, and it displayed "Identity Confirmed: Savannah Marie Curtis." The screen opened to reflect what was being displayed on the monitor.

Each team was assigned a specific project. Their team, Team 12, was tasked on a cream that would assist in the treatment of eczema. Eczema was a condition that generally presented itself in early childhood with chronic itchy, weeping, oozing skin. It tended to be on the hands and forearms of most patients.

A treatment cream had already been developed by WVL, and it was their task to make it better. They went over the project and the basics of what the current version of the cream did and discussed what type of improvements they should be looking for.

In the early afternoon, Artemus asked Marcus what they as interns were being judged on exactly. When he had asked the question, it occurred to Savannah that she had been wondering the same exact thing. From the looks on everyone's faces, she wasn't alone.

Marcus looked around the room, then said, "You are going to be measured on several things. Some I can tell you, and some I cannot. You are going to be judged on both your individual ability and the ability to work with a team to start. Every step of this program is monitored, and it is not recommended that you withhold any information from your team, thinking that will get you ahead. It will reflect poorly should you decide to go rogue and do things on your own. There is a balance between personal goals and the group dynamic, and it is expected you will find it."

As days, then weeks passed, it seemed to Savannah that her team found its stride. Where she was very scientific in her approach, similar to Artemus, Maliek and Michelle had more of an experimentation type of approach. Finding a good balance was interesting between the two methods.

Although Marcus continued to flirt, she quickly came to the realization that that was simply his personality. Him being the mentor of her group, there was no chance of any romantic involvement.

Savannah was pleased that she had seen Charlie a couple times since the internship began. Each time, his amazing smile made her breath catch just a little and her cheeks flush. The third time they "bumped" into each other, of course not as dramatically as the first time, he handed her a white envelope with a little smiley face drawn on it. It read, "I'm still sorry." When she opened it at home that night, she found a $100 gift card to her favorite clothing store, which she had never mentioned to him. There was a note as well that read, "I hope this in some small part makes up for the terrible first impression. I would love to take you out for a drink sometime. I promise not to spill it on you. Charlie."

It took Savannah a little while to decide what to do about the invitation. She was not very good at relationships, having only had two brief ones in her life: one in high school and one in college. Both had lasted under a month, and both had ended by her saying the exact wrong thing and not realizing it until the other person lost interest in talking to her. It hadn't done much for her self-esteem, so she immersed herself in what she knew and could control—school and work.

She had two more encounters with Charlie. She could tell by how awkward those brief moments were that he was looking for his answer, and she managed to stumble through each conversation without giving him one.

Savannah finally decided to get him her own card. She thought about how she would deliver it for over a week. She wanted it to be a cute, romantic gesture. She had even left on earlier than normal each night for a week to watch romantic comedies on Netflix with the hope of getting the right inspiration.

One Friday afternoon, she waited in the café for over an hour around the normal lunchtime hoping to run into him. When he didn't show up, she gave up and started to head back down to the labs. She pressed the button for the elevator, but there was a delay. Frustrated, she swiped her card and pulled open the door to the stairwell. As the door swung open, faster than she was expecting, she realized someone was pushing from the other side. Too late, the momentum caused them to land in a heap on the floor. When she got a look at the person now lying atop her, she found it was Charlie.

She shook her head as she stood up, thinking that this was possibly the worst thing that could happen. Charlie was apologizing and explaining that he had not really been looking where he was headed and hadn't been prepared for the door to open so "violently." Savannah simply held up her hand, just as she had at their first meeting and said, "It's okay, Charlie. I'm the one who should be sorry. Are you okay?"

"Yeah, of course. I'm fine," he replied. His mussed hair and smile dazzled her, making her cheeks begin to flush.

"I was just heading back to the lab," she said and gestured toward the stairs behind her.

"Oh, well then…" He swiped his card, then opened the door for her. "I hope you have an eventful day."

God, he is charming, she thought. "You too," she replied and walked through the now opened door. Just as she began to descend the steps, she heard his voice behind her. "Wait, I think you dropped this." She turned around and he was holding up the card. His card. "Did you drop it?" he asked when she didn't reply.

"No actually…" Her voice was a little shaken. "That's not mine. Well it was mine, but now it isn't. It's… Well, it's yours… so, yeah." Charlie looked at the envelope as Savannah turned on her heels and ran down the stairs without looking back.

I am a total idiot, she thought as she opened the lab door.

"Where have you been?" Maliek asked. Savannah didn't take very many breaks, and when she did, they were usually only about fifteen or so minutes. "I was reading and thinking," she said, sounding more confident than she did with Charlie just moments before.

The team had been working on a theory that if instead of trying to either dry out the sores or irritated skin, maybe they could create a thin coating that would act as a barrier. It would protect the surface of the skin, allowing the skin to heal itself on the thermal level.

They had dug up everything on the subject of eczema and how treatments had worked or failed in the past. Savannah had also gathered quite a bit of information from several support group websites that had more than just clinical or medical views of the affliction. They had the human voice that most clinical research would never contain.

Maliek had programmed a clock into everyone's tablet that counted down the days until the first elimination date. He had taken computer programming as part of his masters, and the clock said that they had 98 days remaining. It was almost 11pm when Savannah finished uploading her research for the night onto everyone's USB. She had purchased one for each team member to make transferring and sharing their research easier. Their tablets were all set up for bio-recognition. Although Maliek had said it was an easy work around, Savannah knew it wouldn't score her or her team any points if they broke the lab's security routines.

She walked to her locker and found an envelope taped to it with her name on it. She pulled it off the locker and read the note inside:

Dear Van,

Thank you for your note and your very cute way of presenting it to me.

I would love to meet you for that drink. Since you are probably reading this sometime after 10pm, you should go home and get some sleep. But I want you to meet me at O'Neil's Pub at 5th and Central tomorrow night at 7pm.

I will be waiting with that drink.

Charlie

Savannah smiled, slipping the note back into its envelope, then tucking it into her bag. She couldn't help but think that the note was the most romantic gesture of her life.

The next day was her day off, and it was nerve wracking. Savannah realized she had no idea how to dress for the date. She didn't know if it was casual or fancy, and she didn't want to make a mistake in either direction. She went through her entire closet and couldn't find anything suitable. As she stood and looked in the mirror, she could only think that she desperately needed a haircut. Savannah had blue eyes, where the rest of her family's had been brown, green, or somewhere in-between. The one thing they did all have in common was carrot top red hair, and hers fell in spiral curls down between her shoulder blades.

Savannah left her apartment and found a cute salon located in the older part of town. She was able to get a manicure and pedicure and get her hair trimmed and styled in a cute ponytail with tendrils that framed her face. She also found a clothing shop two doors down from the salon and bought a blue dress with spaghetti straps that matched her eyes and a pair of strappy sandals. The outfit was casual but nice, and after a little makeup application at her apartment, she looked ready, even if her insides were doing flip flops.

O'Neil's Pub had been a staple in this community for years, and when she entered, it had a comfortable feel. Round, dark wood tables were scattered throughout with a long bar along one wall. At the very back of the restaurant, near the hallway labeled "Privies," was a small stage with a banner that read, "Trivia Night Tonight 8pm."

The hostess approached as she was scanning the tables for any sign of Charlie. Before the hostess could ask her anything, Savannah nearly jumped out of her skin when she heard a voice beside her say, "Who are you looking for so intently?" She turned to see Charlie, his hair in its normal muss, smiling at her.

"Sorry. Didn't mean to startle you." He turned to the hostess and asked, "Table for two, please." Savannah didn't think she could be more nervous, but when the hostess asked if they intended to play trivia tonight, Charlie said, "Yes."

Seated at a table near the middle of the restaurant, they were each handed a menu, and she held hers up, blocking her face and pretended to read it. "Nervous?" Charlie asked after a time.

She partially lowered her menu to see that his was up, also covering his face. "A little," she replied sheepishly.

He lowered his menu and looked directly into her eyes. "Me too."

She righted the menu again, looked it over and decided on lamb stew, then put it down. Charlie put his down as well and looked as if he were going to say something when the waiter stepped up to the table and asked what they would like to drink. Charlie ordered ale from their in-house selection; Savannah ordered water with lemon. The waiter asked if they wanted an appetizer. Charlie looked over to her for guidance, which she wasn't ready to give. "I'm good," she replied.

"We're good," Charlie confirmed. The waiter left after their drinks, and Savannah's gaze wandered to the road signs all over the walls. She could tell they were from Europe, most likely Ireland. "I'm glad you came," Charlie said.

She met his gaze. "Me too."

After a few minutes of silence, she asked, "So, trivia? Are you any good?" with the best smirk she could muster. That caused him to chuckle a bit, and not sure if he was chuckling at her or his own trivia prowess, she added, "I do play a mean Trivial Pursuit game. I hope you're ready." She sounded much more confident than she expected.

Being overly intelligent was a huge turn off for most guys. She hoped that Charlie wasn't one of them. As she looked at his dimple and caramel eyes smiling at her, she decided then that she was going to be herself with him, even if it meant this was the only time he would ask her out. She was working on her life now, her destiny, and she wasn't going to pretend to be anything other than who she was.

"I look forward to the challenge, Ms. Curtis," he replied formally. It made her laugh.

While the drinks arrived and the food was ordered, Charlie asked her all sorts of questions about her life and helped her by answering the same questions about his own. He was originally born in Montana, but his parents had moved to Florida when he was very young. He was an only child. He had been a science nerd in school, which she could relate to. He told her stories of failed experiments in his garage, that he had set the garage on fire three times, and only one of them was more than a small one. He was also proud of the never-ending patience of his parents in his pursuit of knowledge.

She told him all about growing up in the desert, learning everything she could get her hands on, that she loved the research part of science and the feeling there was always a stone to uncover. Savannah told him about her sister and how different they were. That being the youngest she was often compared to her sister, who was more into athletics than academics. She explained that this was her first big move from home, and that sometimes she missed her sister ribbing her about being such a nerd. Charlie listened to everything she said with rapt attention. He seemed interested in what she had to say, even when she rambled.

When the trivia started up, she was surprised at how comfortable Charlie made her feel in their short time together. He moved his chair close to hers so that he could face the stage when the first round began. There were four rounds to the first game with five questions in each round. Charlie handed over the pad that had been provided to her, along with a pen from his pocket. When she twirled it around in her hand, she saw the engraving: "What Is Your Future?"

She looked up at Charlie and thought that she had been right. This was going to be the best year of her life.

The trivia was easy for her except the sports questions. Charlie simply put his arm on the back of her chair and looked over her shoulder at her answers. If there were any she didn't know or seemed to be struggling with, he told her the answer for her to write in. They won every round. At the end of the first game, they were called up on stage to collect their prize, two O'Neil's t-shirts that said, "Yes, I am the smartest person in the room!" and a $25 bar tab. Savannah disliked being in front of crowds, and Charlie seemed to sense it. He put his hand on her back to reassure her that he was right there with her.

After they left the stage, Charlie picked up the tab. She didn't even try to ask to split it. She knew he would just scoff at the idea. "Thank you, Van, for an amazing evening," he said as she hailed a cab.

Nodding, she replied, "My sister calls me Van."

"Oh, sorry. I just thought ... it suits you," he said. "You don't mind, do you?" He looked slightly worried.

"No, it's cute... Chuck," she said and smiled. He gave her a dramatically offended look, which caused her to burst out laughing. He stood there and just looked "pretend mad" as her dad called it when she had pouted as a child.

When she finally stopped giggling, her eyes were watering a little. She wiped them and when she looked up, Charlie stood very close. He opened the door to the cab, and as she was about to step in his hand came up, moved a tendril of hair, and tucked it behind her ear. Then his hand held her chin up, and he leaned down to kiss her. Savannah froze briefly, then as his lips met hers, she melted. He kissed her gently, then pulled back.

He smiled and said, "I think you have my pen, Ms. Curtis. Might you use it to give me your number?" He used the same formal voice he had earlier. She nodded and looked through her purse. She could only find the gift certificate from the pub to write on. She pulled out his pen, wrote her number down, and handed him both her number and the pen.

"Goodnight, Van," he said and lightly kissed her cheek before closing the door to the cab.

It had been a perfect evening!

She replayed the night on the ride back to her apartment, even touching her lips where he had kissed her. It had been so simple and fun. She had never imagined it could be like that. As she lay in her bed that night, thinking about every moment, she felt a nagging thought began to creep across her mind. Charlie was a competitor to her in this challenge. They both could make it to the end, but statistically, she knew that would be difficult. As she fell asleep, she wondered if she was setting herself up for another love life failure.

The next morning she woke up and made herself some toast with cherry jam and a cup of tea. She turned on her laptop to continue her research when her phone went off. It was a text.

[Good morning, did you know that the word Trivia means the joining of three roads in ancient Rome?]

Although she didn't have the number in her phone, she knew it was Charlie.

[Van: Good Morning! Did you know that sometimes gladiator blood was recommended by Roman physicians as an aid to fertility?]

[Charlie: LOL. I want to take you out again soon; you choose the place. Just let me know when and where.]

She read the text several times, then replied, [Okay, deal!] and knew there was no pressure.

They kept up their busy work schedules, adjusting slightly to make time for each other. The sacrifice of the time, she always thought, was worth it for Charlie. He was fun, and it gave her a part of life she hadn't experienced before. The first few weeks she thought she would screw it up at any moment, but he seemed to really get her and never seemed put off or annoyed.

They fell into a routine. They would have a late dinner and watch a movie on Wednesday nights, and they would have a date night on Friday nights. Sunday mornings were reserved for relaxing and doing something outdoors. Savannah was amazed how it worked and they just fit. They never spoke about work except to ask how each other's day was. There was an unspoken understanding that discussing work was off limits.

It was nearing the end of the first six months when Savannah made an interesting discovery. There was some fruit from the jungles of South America called the Jambu. The red fruit was sweet and edible, but the white fruit possessed an acidic quality that natives thought was poisonous. The leaves from this fruit-bearing plant possessed a leather like quality, and it was this combination that the team was looking for. Savannah ordered samples to test her theory before she presented it to the team. She didn't want to send them on a wild goose chase when they were so close to the end of round one, and two of the team would be leaving. She knew the pressure weighed heavily on all of them.

The plants arrived the week before the first elimination round. Savannah stayed later than normal almost every night that week. She didn't miss her time with Charlie; some small part of her wasn't sure what would happen if either one of them didn't make the first round.

On Thursday night, she was on the last step with the plant samples. She mixed it with most of the parts of the refined formula for the cream the team had been working on. The change was astounding. It caused the cream to form a barrier that was almost impenetrable. She documented her findings and each step, including pictures.

She wasn't sure if it was the breakthrough they were looking for, but it would need further testing. The team could work on it the next day. She did one final test on batch of mice with eczema, placing some of the new cream on the affected areas, separated them to a different cage, and secured the container. She loaded up everyone's USB and closed up the lab for the night.

The next morning, when she arrived at the lab, there was a security guard standing outside the door. When she tried to enter, he stopped her and informed her that no one was allowed to enter. She and her team were to report to conference room 4. She returned to her locker, hung up her lab coat, and grabbed her bag. A lump formed in the pit of her stomach.

She made her way to conference room four and found Artemus pacing at the back of the room. He looked over when she walked in. "Savannah, what happened last night?" he asked, his voice near panic.

"Nothing," she replied. "I was working a bit with a plant sample, but everything was fine when I left," she said. Her heart sank. The mice, she thought.

She sat down, her elbows on the table and her head in her hands. What have I done? Her other teammates finally arrived, as bewildered as she had been. They all speculated on what was happening, and Savannah didn't know if or what she should say. She was about to explain about the plant when Marcus walked through the doors, followed by Mr. Handleson, the head of the internship program. The room fell silent.

"Ms. Curtis, please come with me," Mr. Handleson said.

Savannah got up, and grabbing her bag, she started walking toward the door with her head hanging. She was done; she knew it. Mr. Handleson opened the door for her and immediately followed her out. He led her down a series of hallways, but she wasn't focusing on where she was being taken. All she could think was that she had just blown her life apart. Her chest got tight when he finally stopped before a door, swiped his card, and gestured for her to enter.

They entered an office that overlooked the courtyard and fountains. "Please, have a seat." He gestured to an empty chair in front of his desk. "Can I get you some coffee, water, or a soda?" he asked politely, motioning to the mini-bar located on the back corner of the room. She shook her head.

"Ms. Curtis, may I call you Savannah?" he asked. She nodded. She was starting to feel lightheaded. "As you may have surmised, we had a problem in the lab last night." He was looking at her now.

"I am so sorry..." she began to say. He held up his hand for silence.

"Ms. Curtis, as I'm sure you are aware, all lab activity is monitored," he continued. "What you did last night was extraordinary."

"Wait... what?" she said. Am I hearing him correctly?

"What you did last night was extraordinary," he repeated. "Oh, Savannah, I apologize for how this must look. You're not in any trouble. In fact, quite the opposite."

It took her a moment to take in what he was saying. He went on to explain that each team had, in fact, been given the same project and that two of the teams had actually made progress and changed properties of the cream. It occurred to her that she didn't know what team Charlie was on. She hoped he was on one of those teams.

Mr. Handleson continued, explaining that when she'd ordered the plant samples, they had been somewhat stumped until they looked at the experiments she was conducting. The formula had the effect, in a manner, which she had intended it to. It caused a barrier that made the skin impervious to the absorption of any foreign substances; however, it was still allowing air through.

It was an exciting breakthrough, and they wanted her to continue her line of research. "Does that mean I am moving on to the next phase of the program?" she asked.

He chuckled. "Not exactly. We'd like to offer you a position at WVL. It's entry level, but here." He handed her a folder similar to the one she'd received on her first day. "Look this over and let us know what you think."

She sat and looked down at the envelope. She was being offered a position after only six months. It was unheard of. She closed her eyes and shook her head a little as if that would clear away the unreal feeling. When she opened her eyes, the silver WVL logo was shining back up at her from the folder she held. She moved her chair closer to the desk and opened the packet. It was a similar contract to the one she signed when she had started the internship program. However, this one was offering her a three-year contract, a great starting salary, and a small profit-sharing incentive. It was her dream.

She grabbed a pen from the holder on the desk. It was silver, the same pen given to them on their first day and the same pen she used to give Charlie her number. With the pen poised above the paper, she hesitated. What if Charlie doesn't make it?

"Is there a problem, Savannah?" Mr. Handleson asked.

"No. Actually, I have a question," she said. "Will the program continue?"

Mr. Handleson nodded. "Yes, it will. There are still two positions to fill. Your role at WVL is in a different area than was intended for those completing the internship."

She felt a sense of relief wash over her. "Am I able to discuss this offered position with my close friends and family?" she asked.

Mr. Handleson nodded again. "Yes, of course, as long as you use discretion. The teams are being culled today and those that remain will discover soon enough that you have taken on a new role."

She signed a copy of the contract, handed it over to him, and replaced the pen in the holder. He told her it would be best if she took the rest of the day off to ready herself for her new position on Monday. He walked her to Personnel and helped her get her new employee badge, be assigned a parking space assignment, and fill out the remaining paperwork.

It was a little after 1pm when she finally left. She called her parents first, then her sister. They were all thrilled for her. Her parents didn't ask about Charlie. They knew how the program worked and that there was a chance he wouldn't get accepted. Her sister asked however, and Savannah had to tell her that she didn't know yet. Charlie had insisted that they have a movie in the park date that night to celebrate their advancement. Only then would she know what happened to Charlie, when she met him under their favorite tree at eight that night.

She got home and found she couldn't concentrate. She wanted to call or text him, but they had agreed that life was to go on as normal. She found herself cleaning her entire apartment from top to bottom. She was almost late getting ready when she finally looked at the time again.

She wore jeans and the O'Neil's shirt they had won on their first trivia night. They had won again a few times, but that shirt was special to her. She needed it close as she walked up to the tree, blanket in hand. Charlie was already there with a cooler of treats. She looked at him, taking him all in. She knew that no matter what happened, she had something truly amazing with him. He was wearing the same O'Neil's shirt she had on. In that moment, she knew she loved him.

She moved toward him, dropping the blanket and throwing her arms around his neck, kissing him deeply. She needed to feel him close to her. He wrapped his arms around her waist. They stood, frozen in time. She pulled back when she realized she had tears streaming down her face and rested her forehead against his chest, their arms still around each other.

"Tell me, please..." she whispered.

"I made it," he said, then kissed her forehead.

She smiled and kissed him again. After letting him hold her close for a moment, she wiped the tears from her cheeks and went to grab the blanket. They sat under their tree and had another perfect night together. She had landed her dream job and her dream man.

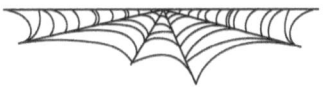

When she arrived for work on Monday, nothing could dampen her elation.

She took the map from her pocket and reconfirmed the location of her new office. It was located on the 3rd basement floor, the restricted area.

She entered the elevator and pushed the button for the 3rd level. When she did, a red light shot out from the sensor and moved across the room. A pad slid from the wall with a finger-print scanner. She placed her finger on the reader, and it flashed green and withdrew into the wall as the elevator began moving. She found out later that if anyone was on the elevator without level three clearance, the elevator would not descend.

She arrived at her assigned lab and saw it had a similar set up to the one she had been working in for the last six months.

She had the same tablet with all her previous research, and in addition, she had a large monitor that was a touch screen. She could use her tablet or touch screen directly. Fancy, she thought. Maliek would be in heaven.

She opened her tablet to find a file with a video. It was Dr. Burness, someone she recognized from a video shown at orientation, one of the Directors of the Research and Development team.

The video explained that they were expecting her to continue with the research she was doing and to report back when she stabilized the formula. He indicated that she should see three new icons on her tablet. Two were internal/external research pathways now at her disposal. The third was reporting software for her to log the progress of her project. All three had a tutorial and would be fairly easy for her to navigate. At the end of the video, he let her know if there was anything she needed she was to let him know. He wished her good luck, and the video ended.

Savannah continued to keep the same schedule as Charlie and cherished every moment. As she rode into work one morning, she couldn't help but think that she had done it. She was one of the lucky ones. In the blink of an eye, it seemed another six months passed.

The days that led up to the next decision day brought with them a heavy rock that sat in Savannah's stomach. As per usual, Charlie wouldn't discuss it.

On Friday, the day of the eliminations, she heard a tapping at her lab door. Standing outside was one of the guards. He was holding a glass vase with several glass flowers, and as he handed it over, he pulled a card from his pocket. "Someone must like you," he said, then returned to his post.

She set the vase down. There was a metal plate that was engraved with "TOGETHER WE WILL CHANGE THE FUTURE," the company motto on the welcome sign. She opened the card. "You can stop worrying now—Charlie." She released a breath she hadn't even know she had been holding as a huge smile crept across her face. She looked more closely at the glass flowers. He had gotten her something she could always look at—they could be sterilized.

A few weeks later, she was asked to present the current state of her research and her findings to date.

She was surprised to find over ten people seated around the conference table when she arrived. She had assumed it was just going to be Dr. Burness and maybe a couple others. Ten was almost overwhelming.

"Ms. Curtis, I assume you are ready?" Dr. Burness said.

She moved to the front of the room and, using the large touch-screen monitor, logged in. She walked through her entire presentation. There were a few questions, but most of the audience just listened. When she concluded, she stood waiting.

Dr. Burness was having a whispered conversation with someone to his left. With a start, Savannah recognized him. It was Dr. Sidelinger. Her heart began to race. Her hands began to sweat, and she looked down, shifting the tablet so she didn't drop it.

"Very impressive, Ms. Curtis," said Dr. Sidelinger. "Please come by my office this afternoon at three to discuss the next phase of your research." She nodded as he stood and left, the rest of the room following suit.

She was early for the meeting, but Dr. Sidelinger beckoned her to come in and to take a seat. She attempted to portray an air of calm, despite her rapidly beating heart.

"Ms. Curtis, I want to say again how impressed I am with what you have accomplished in such a short amount of time," he began. "I would like you to know that your research, from all appearances, has an application that we would like you to look into further. We have a project of a very sensitive nature. We would like you to make certain modifications. You will be enlightened on the specifics you need as the project progresses. Are you interested?"

It took her a moment to notice he was waiting for her to respond. Nodding again, she said, "Yes, yes, absolutely."

"Good. I am glad to hear that. You will receive your instructions starting tomorrow; this project is of the highest confidentiality. You may discuss it only with Dr. Burness and myself. Is that understood?" he asked in a more serious tone.

"Yes, perfectly understood, sir," she replied.

"I look forward to your results then," he said as he walked her to the door.

She didn't discover for two days what the next phase of her research meant. First, she was moved to a deeper part of the building; unbeknownst to her there was a fourth floor to the basement. It was really floor 3.5 as it wasn't entirely under the third floor. There was a larger lab that had a doorway that led down a short flight of stairs to the more secure area. A person had to have two bio scans, eye and fingerprint, and voice recognition to enter. There were pressurized doors at every point of entry.

As she became acclimated to her new environment, she discovered that this area was entirely independent from the rest of the building. The ventilation and environmental controls were completely self-contained. When Dr. Burness gave her the tour, she saw that each of the labs had glass that darkened when the lab was occupied.

Savannah was surprised to see the high level of security in this type of facility. She assumed that this type of set up would be reserved for military facilities. Dr. Burness chuckled a little when she asked during the tour. Each project was classified, he said, and only those on the project were to discuss it.

When she was shown to her new office, she saw that everything from her lab, including Charlie's flowers, had been transported to her new location.

The next day she was given her first task. The cream she had designed created a barrier that protected the skin from outside elements, water and air notwithstanding. Her task was to make it so that the cream could be translated into gas form.

It wasn't an easy undertaking; however, she was given no deadlines and no apparent pressure. She worked tirelessly, sending in her reports daily. Occasionally, she would receive a note that gave her an idea to try to assist her. After sixty-four days, she had her third successful trial.

The next day, Dr. Burness asked her to bring one of her specimens to test in his lab. She readied one of the rats she had been given for this purpose, and when she entered, he took the specimen and placed it into a container that had three levels of seals. Once it was inside, he pressed a control on his tablet, and she heard the sound of air being moved. A light mist began to fall within the container.

At first, the rat seemed fine, but after a several minutes, she saw that it was having some difficulty. Its skin began to turn color, and it started to have seizures. The seizures did not last long before all movement ceased.

Savannah covered her mouth; she'd never seen anything like it before.

"Ms. Curtis, I need you to make your formula stronger, less susceptible to airborne intrusion," Dr. Burness said without looking away from the specimen.

"What was that?" she heard herself ask.

"Classified," he said, adding no further context.

She returned to her lab, slightly dazed, and when she got there, she searched for anything related to what she saw that day. There was nothing in the research files.

When she got home that night, she started her search again. She couldn't find anything specific as it related to WVL, but she found pictures that resembled what she had seen in the lab. They were pictures of victims of bio-weapons. She shook her head. That couldn't be right.

At lunch the next day, she sought out Marcus. He had a very standard schedule for lunch, and she knew she was likely to find him. When she approached the table, he smiled up at her. "Well, if it isn't the ginger genius," he said, gesturing for her to take a seat. "What can I do you for, Savannah?" he asked.

"How are you?" she asked. "How is the team?"

He shook his head. "When you were ... transferred, the team was disbanded at the first round of the program. Michelle didn't make it to round two; Artemus didn't make it to round three. That left Maliek, and he is on the team with your friend Charlie," he said, using his fingers as quotes when he said "friend."

Since she and Charlie never discussed work, she wasn't that surprised she didn't know who his teammates were. "You don't happen to have Maliek's number, do you?" she asked.

He narrowed his eyes for a moment, then said, "No, but since he is right over there, why don't you ask him yourself?" He pointed to the window where Maliek sat.

"Thanks," she said.

Maliek jumped a little when she tapped him on the shoulder. When he saw her, he smiled. "Well, if it isn't the smartest girl in the room."

"Hi, how are you?" she asked and pointed to the seat beside him. "May I?"

He nodded and replied, "I have been good. A little worried about that last round, but good. What do they have you doing?" he asked. "Wait, never mind. I know you can't tell me. So, what brings you topside with us interns?"

Savannah looked around, then leaned in and whispered, "I need your help actually. When we were working together, you mentioned that you saw some of the icons that were … hidden … during the internship."

"Yes," he said, looking puzzled.

She sighed and continued, "I was just curious how you were able to see them because I somehow hid two of mine, and well, I feel a little silly. Since I would've asked Dr. Burness… I was hoping you could help me so…"

"So you don't look dumb in front of your new boss?" he finished for her.

She felt herself flush because she was lying, and she hated it. But since he thought she was embarrassed, she played on it. "Yes. Can you… Will you help me please?" she asked.

He wrapped his arm around her shoulders and said, "Only if you remember us little people when you are a big deal around here."

She smiled up at him and nodded. "How could I ever forget?"

Maliek could explain how to find the hidden icons in a few minutes. It wasn't that it was a simple process; it was his ease explaining it. She walked through it with him twice to ensure she had it exactly and thanked him.

When she got back to the lab, she went through her normal steps while she thought about what she should do.

After a week or so of debating, she convinced herself that she was overreacting. She continued her work and made progress on Dr. Burness's request.

A month later, she was ready for the next test. She brought, as requested, two specimens: one that had been treated right before the test and one treated the night before.

When she brought them into Dr. Burness's lab, she began to feel uneasy. Seeing the same set up as before, the nagging voice in her head was shouting that she had buried what she didn't want to see instead of looking at it.

The test was run on both rats. The rat that had been treated right before the test lasted about ten minutes longer than the last one, but the rat treated the night before fared much better, lasting an additional forty-five minutes before it started to show symptoms.

She cleared her throat as Dr. Burness made some notes. "Excuse me, Dr. Burness? Perhaps if I understood exactly what it was I was trying to make the project resistant to, I could make more progress in the direction needed," she said as diplomatically as possible.

"It's CLASSIFIED, Ms. Curtis. Please do not ask again," he scolded. She left his lab without another word.

When she returned to her lab, she went right back into her research and continued to look for the longevity they were after in her "project." When the labs were empty and she had turned in her report for the night, she sat and looked at the vase of glass flowers for a long time. She was supposed to meet Charlie that night, but she wasn't sure she could face him. She wanted nothing more than to hide in his arms, but she knew she had to discover what her research was being used for.

She grabbed her tablet and followed Maliek's instructions exactly. Surprisingly, she could access the confidential files. She started with Dr. Burness's project. Reading through the reports, she began to feel physically ill. The more she read, project after project, the more sickened she was by what she saw.

Later, as she sat on the floor and hugged a plastic container that contained all the contents of her stomach, she began to weep. She felt lost for the first time in a very long time. She was alone and scared. She sat there for some time and simply stared at nothing. Eventually, she tried to will herself to become numb. She assumed that was what the others around her must have done.

Knowledge is power, she thought. But she didn't know what to do with this knowledge. After hours of considering every option, she could only think of one. She got up, cleaned up her lab, closed down her tablet, and left for the night.

She took a cab to his apartment. She and Charlie had never spoken about work, and as she walked up the steps, she realized she wasn't sure how to explain. She hesitated on the landing, his door looming before her.

What if he is fine with it? What if to him it doesn't matter? He isn't supposed to know. Telling him anything puts him in danger of losing everything. I would be taking his dream.

She had turned to leave when the door behind her opened. "Van?" Charlie called from the doorframe. She quickly wiped the tears from her face and turned around. "Oh, baby, are you okay?" He moved toward her.

"Yeah. I'm good. Just a hard day," she said, her voice a little shaky. "I came to say I'm sorry for... I mean... about tonight. I missed our date..." She forced a small smile. He pulled her into his arms, and the moment her head hit his shoulder, she felt the tears begin.

He pulled back to give her a soft kiss on her forehead and walked her inside. He guided her to the couch and sat with her as she cried, not saying a word, just brushing the strands of hair from her face and planting soft kisses on her head with his arms wrapped around her.

The next morning, Savannah woke up to Charlie gently shaking her awake. As her eyes focused, she saw the sun was streaming in through the sliding glass doors in the living room.

"I made you some coffee and a bagel," Charlie said. He gestured to a plate and mug on the coffee table before her.

She sat up and asked, "What happened?"

"You cried for a while and then you were out. You seemed really tired so I didn't want to wake you. But since it is Friday, I figured we both needed to get up. After all, today is the day!" he said at last with a little smirk.

She brushed her hands against her face and pulled the hair back from her eyes. Today was the day. The end of round three. She looked at the food before her and felt sick all over again. She got up and went to the bathroom.

As she stared in the mirror, she knew she wasn't going to say anything to Charlie. She wasn't going to say anything at all. The perfection of her life with him would not be ruined by this.

She splashed water on her face, brushed her teeth, and headed back to the living room. Charlie had put her coffee in a travel cup and had her bagel all wrapped. "I know you have to run," he said with a smile.

She threw her arms around his neck. "You're kinda perfect, Mr. Miller," she said and kissed him deeply. "I will see you tonight to celebrate." Grabbing the coffee and bagel, she headed out the door.

Savannah slowed her pace as she walked up to the glass double doors of WVL. She remembered the first time seeing them and the feeling she had. She smiled when she remembered Charlie and how they met. Walking into her lab, she looked around at the place she once saw as her future. Now, only the glass flowers held any value.

She took her time, constructing her last words to Charlie. She wanted him to know that what he had given her meant the world, and that what she was doing was because she wanted a world where he wouldn't have to be a part of her choices or why she was making them. When she finished, she hit send. She knew he wouldn't check his email until after he was done for the day. By then it would be too late.

She walked to the room that housed the containers carrying what she needed. Carefully, she removed what she was looking for. It was early in the afternoon, and she knew the labs were fully staffed.

She walked to the entry room atop the stairs. She sealed the doors and set down the vase of glass flowers. She read the inscription one more time. "TOGETHER WE WILL CHANGE THE FUTURE." She was doing just that, changing the future, she thought, and smiled. With a deep breath, she opened the first container and let the gas seep into the air.

AFTER THE BLACKNESS

When Savannah's body began to spasm, Charlie pulled off the hood and gloves of his suit and pulled her onto his lap. He continued to hold her, cradling her now lifeless form against him. After reading her email, there had been a small part of him that had held out hope that this hadn't been her plan. He knew, as he looked at her now, her expression no longer pained, that this was exactly what she wanted.

He held her as close as possible, refusing to let go; he knew if he did, he would have to admit she was gone. He started to feel the effects of what Savannah had unleashed begin to take hold. Charlie laid Savannah down gently as fresh tears streamed down his face. He began to cough and his body began to spasm, but he managed to pull a small box from his pocket and remove the ring. He slid it on her finger, then lay down behind her. He closed his eyes and again pulled her into his embrace.

He wrapped his hand in hers and watched the light glint off the ring and the engraved letters that read, "You are my Future."

MOLLY

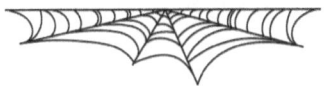

Paul sat at the table in his kitchen staring into his bowl of soggy cereal. He closed his eyes for a moment and remembered when he would wake to the smell of an amazing breakfast being prepared.

He would come into the kitchen, and Ivy would have breakfast all ready before he had to run out the door to an "important" meeting at work—the kind of meeting he had every morning—but they didn't seem nearly as important now.

He could see her standing at the sink in a pair of shorts and the tank top that she liked to sleep in. She would be singing the words of a song that she would say was rolling around in her head for some time. Ivy would say that singing it out loud would cause it to stop being stuck in her head. Paul was never quite sure if the logic was sound, why the beautiful woman before him didn't have to be.

Ivy loved musicals. When he would ask her which song it was that she was singing, she would laugh and tell him the name as if should remember. *I should have remembered,* he thought, opening his eyes.

Ivy had started "dragging" him to shows when they were still dating. Paul had gone, knowing that she loved them, and she would go to every sporting event he asked her too without complaint. She even learned what the plays meant, what they were called, who the teams were, and even the names of the players. She had an amazing memory.

He opened his eyes. Staring into the bowl before him, he found he had stirred his spoon around enough that it had mushed the soggy flakes into an even more liquefied state. Ivy would not have wanted him to be sitting here feeling guilty about not knowing the title song to the musical Chicago. She would have smiled, told him how adorable he was, and kissed his forehead.

Before he could sink deeper into his guilt, his phone beeped. A text message.

It was his secretary reminding him to bring in the Drabrough proposal. The meeting on it was today. He had worked on it for the last two months. He had been chasing the deal for the last couple of years, and this was the moment.

Drabrough Manufacturing had been shopping around for a place to build their largest manufacturing plants to date. Paul had this one opportunity to have them choose the East Coast and close the largest deal of his career.

He texted a reply, put his bowl in the sink, and headed out. He would stop for coffee on the way in. He hadn't figured out how to use the fancy French press that Ivy had made the most amazing coffee in each morning before work.

When he began to pull out of garage and into the driveway, he spotted a small pink plastic car in the rear-facing camera in his dashboard.

He put the car in park, opened the door, and got out. The pink "car" belonged to his neighbor's daughter. She was four and rode the motorized car around as if she were a race car driver. She always had a stuffed dog in the seat next to her.

Paul gave a small smile, remembering her driving up and down the sidewalk when he and Ivy would sit on the front porch on a Saturday morning enjoying a cup of coffee. Then his smile faded, and he tried to turn on the car to steer it out of the way. The battery was dead, so he was only able to push it onto his lawn. He knew Marci or Ben would be over to grab it soon enough to get it charged back up.

Paul got back in the car and headed to work. There had been enough memories for one morning. He had heard the cliché that "Time heals all wounds." He wished that someone could tell him the amount of time he could wait to heal the wound he had. It was deep and hurt constantly.

Ivy had died on a Sunday.

Paul had received the call from Barbara his mother-in-law on Friday night. Ivy had started bleeding. She had been taken by ambulance to Trinity Memorial Hospital in critical condition. Barbara had tried to explain more, but Paul only heard his pulse in his ears as his heart felt like it was going to burst from his chest. He got on the next flight he could which was a redeye. He had been in California on a "team building" weekend for his firm.

He arrived at the hospital at 8:47am to find Ivy in ICU. He wasn't allowed in the room. He was looking at her lying in the hospital bed, and the only thing he could recognize about his wife was the color of the hair splayed across the pillow where her head rested.

He leaned against the window, trying to will himself into the room through the window. He wanted her to at least know he was there... by her side.

As he looked at all the tubes and monitors sticking out of the only girl he had ever loved, tears started to run down his face.

He heard a voice in his head screaming to not give up, that she would be okay, that they would both be okay. But there was that part of him, the dark part that saw the scene unfolding before him, that knew she wasn't going to leave that room.

Paul felt a hand on his shoulder as he closed his eyes to pull himself out of where he was headed mentally.

It was Barbara, his mother-in-law. Her husband Roy was just behind her standing stoically. Roy had been part of a generation of men who didn't cry in front of others. Any grief he was feeling, any pain, he would bear alone.

Paul turned and hugged Barbara, pulling her close. She hugged him back, rubbing his back the way she would comfort a child.

"The doctor will return soon and needs to speak with you, Paul," she said, almost as a whisper.

He pulled back from the embrace and nodded as he let his gaze wander again into the room and to Ivy.

It was only a moment before he heard an unfamiliar male voice behind him. "Mr. Matheson?" Paul turned to see a man about his height and age. He knew instantly it must be the doctor Barbara had spoken of and reached out his hand in greeting. The doctor shook it and introduced himself, "I am Dr. Stephens. I am glad you are here, Mr. Matheson."

"Paul. Call me Paul," he told the doctor.

"Paul. Would you like to sit?" The doctor's voice was very calm, and his demeanor was just as mild. This should have calmed the voice that Paul was hearing in his head, but it seemed to only fuel his fears. Paul wrapped his arms around his chest as if he were suddenly cold. "Paul..." the doctor said, gesturing toward some chairs.

"I'm fine here. Thanks... What... When can I see her?" His thoughts were scrambled and his voice almost pleading. Barbara patted him on the back as she and Roy walked away to give him his privacy.

"Paul, your wife, Ivy suffered a miscarriage. This resulted in tremendous blood loss. When the emergency team arrived, she was not responsive," the doctor continued. "She had what is referred to in medical terms as a Class IV Hemorrhage. Effectively she lost over 40% of the blood volume in her body."

"What do you mean?" Paul asked, suddenly confused. "Ivy wasn't pregnant."

The doctor again stood calmly waiting for Paul to come to terms with the news. When it seemed to sink in, Paul asked, "She lost 40% of the blood in her body?"

Dr. Stephens' response was in the same calm tone. "Simply put, yes. Ivy appears to have begun a miscarriage several days ago. She may not have even known. Spotting and a slight fever are normal in some women, even on their period, which might be why she wasn't aware she was pregnant. However, an infection formed within the tissue in her uterus. Due to this infection, when the bleeding increased, her body was unable to create the necessary clotting to stop it."

Paul was frozen. He was hearing the words, hearing their meaning, but he couldn't make it real. Paul tried to remember the last thing Ivy had said to him. He couldn't remember. He shook his head and looked back to the doctor with the hope that he would tell him the part where Ivy would recover.

"Due to the blood loss, your wife Ivy went into a coma as her vital organs began to shut down."

"What?" Paul said, knowing he had actually heard what the doctor had said.

"Ivy was effectively brain dead for over 20 minutes. Unfortunately, although she received a transfusion, she will not recover."

Paul began to feel lightheaded. He reached out his hand to steady himself against the wall. This wasn't happening. It couldn't be. He looked back at the doctor, ready to ask if there was anything that could be done. He knew the answer, but a part of him couldn't accept that she was gone. As if sensing his question, the doctor slowly shook his head.

Paul moved toward the chairs now and sat. The doctor said something about giving him a minute. Paul pulled out his phone to look at the last texts he had received from her the night before.

[Ivy: Wish you were here to bring me ice cream and rub my feet]

[Ivy: I love you, PBJ]

Ivy had called him PBJ since their first date. It was supposed to be an amazing romantic picnic. They had gotten rained out just as they had set up the picnic. Ivy had invited him over to her place to dry off. They had made peanut butter and jelly sandwiches and watched JAWS on TV, commercials and all. It had been perfect in the end. She had been perfect.

It was hard to find a starting point to what had to happen next. Ivy was lying in the bed in the room next to where he was sitting, and at the same time, she wasn't. Looking at the person hooked up to all the machines, Paul felt so many emotions at the same time he thought he would break. But hope was the worst of them, some small irrational part of him that he could barely feel thought she would open her eyes. She would get better.

Dr. Stephens had introduced him to colleague named Dr. Hayes to help both Paul and Ivy's family to get through this time.

Dr. Hayes suggested to Paul to let Ivy's closest friends know what was happening. The doctor said that it would help Paul to have others sharing in this time of loss. It would also give a closure that only being afforded the change to say goodbye could give.

Paul had started with Ivy's friend Sarah; she was Ivy's friend since childhood. When he called, he found he didn't even have the words to explain. When she answered, he began to cry again. He ended up hanging up and texting Sarah the important details. It seemed easier. He did that to the few people that he knew would have to say goodbye.

Paul's parents had arrived later that evening. He had texted them and gotten no reply earlier. It turned out Ivy's parents had called them when it happened. By the end of that day, he was surrounded by those closest to him and Ivy. He felt completely alone.

It was 1:13am when Dr. Hayes patted Paul on the shoulder. The doctor told Paul that everyone had said their goodbyes. Paul nodded.

It took him a few more minutes to head toward the room. He had tried earlier to see her, after Ivy's family had gone into the room, but he knew he wasn't ready. Even now, he wasn't ready.

The doctor had explained that even though there was no brain activity that Ivy could still experience pain. What had happened, what was happening was incredibly painful, and although they were feeding painkillers as part of the treatment, there was no way to know what she was feeling right now.

Paul knew this wasn't about what he was feeling. However, he wanted time to figure out the perfect thing to say, something that would have made Ivy smile while tears streamed down her face. He was capable of doing that when he'd asked her to marry him. He had planned the whole thing for months. He had months. Now he only had minutes, minutes to tell the person who meant everything to him goodbye.

As he entered the room, he could hear the hum and beeping of the machines. He could look at the displays and see her heartbeat move across the screen. That little voice of hope again started to creep in to say that she would and could get up. He sat in the chair that had been placed next to the bed. He picked up her hand. It was warm. He remembered how she would sometimes sneak up behind him when he was working and rub her cold fingertips on this neck. Now, they were warm.

Paul sat, holding his wife's hand, not knowing how much time had passed. He tried to start talking at least 10 times and couldn't get any words to come. He did know how to tell her that this wasn't supposed to happen, he wasn't ready to lose her, and he didn't know how he would live without her. All he could think was that this moment wasn't about him. It was about her, and he didn't know what to say.

He was staring at the horizon-themed wall border that was around every room when he heard the first alarm go off on the machine to his left. He heard motion behind him as he tried to see what was happening. Where was the heartbeat line? A nurse pushed him kindly but firmly away from the bed, saying something about stepping out of the room. He didn't want to let go.

Ivy died at 3:04am.

Paul pulled into his driveway at 10pm. The Drabrough Proposal had been a hit. He had won the bid and his team had gone out to celebrate. This was the largest deal he had closed, and it meant a promotion. At work, he could go through all the motions, and he could make things happen. It was when he wasn't at work anymore that he was alone again.

As he pulled up to the house, he saw that the pink Jeep was still on his lawn. He pulled into the garage and closed it. Grabbing his laptop bag, he went into the house, set the bag on the couch, and went out the front door.

He needed to grab the mail anyhow, and he was surprised that the Jeep was still there. He grabbed the mail and looked over toward the neighbor's house. Their lantern-shaped porch light was still on and so was the one in the living room. He could see it through the curtains. Although a little late, he didn't think that Marci or Ben would mind.

Paul went up to the Jeep. He began to pick it up. It was heavy, but he could use the back wheels to roll it across the yard. He found however it was charged up, and he was able to steer it over unlike this morning.

A little puzzled, Paul knocked on the door. Marci answered, "Hi Paul. Is everything okay?" she asked. Marci and Ben were in their mid-thirties. Marci was a stay-at-home mother and blogger. Ben was an engineer.

"I'm fine. I was just returning..." he said, gesturing at the Jeep. "I found it on my lawn and figured it should be inside."

Marci thanked him and called for Ben to come move the Jeep inside the garage. "I am actually glad you stopped by. I have something for you."

Paul thought it might be a piece of mail delivered to the wrong address and instead it was a folded piece of construction paper.

Paul looked down, then heard Marci say, "Molly made it for you. She said to give it to you today."

Paul gave a small smile. "Tell her I said thank you."

"I will. If you need anything, Ben and I are here," Marci said. He just nodded. That was what most people had said to him over the last few months.

"Goodnight," he said to both of them as Ben returned from putting up the Jeep. They both said goodnight back, and he headed back to the house with his mail and the paper he had just been given in hand.

When he got inside, he threw the mail on the kitchen counter, then changed into his PJ bottoms and a t-shirt. As he was walking back into, he then switched on the TV and went into the kitchen to grab a drink.

He took the cup that had been sitting in the sink. It was the same one he used every night. He rinsed it and put a few ice cubes, then filled it to the top with whiskey. This had become Paul's ritual. He took his first swig and shook his head a little. He had become everything they told you not to when you lose someone.

Dr. Hayes told him it was part of the grieving process, that as long as he kept working and getting better to not worry. Paul liked Dr. Hayes, and he had decided to seek some help when he couldn't sleep during the first week. His first call had been to get some kind of pills that would knock him out. Dr. Hayes would only prescribe if Paul were willing to see him at least once a week. Paul agreed.

Dr. Hayes had helped. Paul could talk to him when he felt as if there was no one else. Paul knew there were others: his family, her family, and their friends. He wasn't ready to share her with them just yet.

He sat before the TV and let it take him places. He usually stuck to action and horror movies, anything without titillating sex scenes, romance, or musical numbers.

He got up to get his second glass when he noticed the folded piece of paper on the counter. He smiled and opened it. He read it at first and shook his head, thinking he must be a little drunker than he thought, although one cup was usually only good for a slight buzz now.

It was a picture of a smiling yellow sun with a rainbow behind it and it said: "Bee Happy."

He crumpled the paper and threw it in the trash. He didn't know what about it upset him exactly, but he grabbed the bottle off the counter and headed back to forget again.

He woke up to the sound of the alarm going off on his phone. He found the bottle lying beside him on the couch. His head was pounding. He debated calling in, but after yesterday's win, there would be a ton of work to do, and if he stayed home, it wouldn't end up being rest.

He took several ibuprofen and got into a hot shower. When he was dressed, he decided to pick up something on the way in. Paul knew that diving into his job would offer a reprieve which he needed. He spent the next couple of nights at work until the wee hours. He only went home to sleep and change his clothes. He didn't need the bottle those nights because he was exhausted when he walked in the door.

He checked his phone as he headed out on Friday night finally. He decided to head home around 11pm. There were two voicemails: one from Ivy's mother Barbara and the other from Dr. Hayes' office. The latter he assumed was to confirm his appointment first thing Monday morning.

Paul found Mondays worked best to help him deal with the week. He verified and deleted. The next one he waited to get home to read.

As he pulled into the driveway, he saw the Jeep was again sitting on his front porch. He looked over, but the lights were out next door. He pulled his car in, then went out and moved the Jeep into his garage so it wouldn't disappear during the night. He closed the garage door and headed inside.

When he woke up the next morning, the sun was already bright in the sky. He checked his phone, seeing it was close to 10am. He used to hate sleeping in on weekends. It seemed like there was always something to do. Now, it seemed like it helped eat up time.

He checked his phone, and there was another voicemail from Barbara. He decided to check to see if something was wrong. The first one he listened to was the most recent. Barbara was just asking him to call and let them know he was alright, that she hadn't intended on offending him if she had.

He listened to the other message.

Barbara was asking Paul if he needed help to pack up Ivy's things. That she understood he needed time. Ivy would have wanted her clothes donated to help a local charity and some of the other items friends and family had asked about.

Paul called her back as he made a pot of coffee, a feat he had finally managed, and pulled a bowl of cereal.

When she answered, he told her he was fine. She didn't ask about the stuff. Barbara was polite like that. She would wait until he said something, so he did. He told her he wasn't ready to go through the stuff just yet. He told her that he would soon, within the month. Dr. Hayes had said it was better to go through it sooner rather than later. Barbara said she was willing to help with anything he needed. He thanked her and said he would call soon with a day.

He ate as the coffee brewed, and when it was done, he headed out to the porch to take in the morning. Dr. Hayes had him start doing this each Saturday about three months ago. The good doctor had told him that if he avoided everything that had to do with Ivy then he was not confronting his grief. He was right. So every Saturday now, he sat on the front porch and drank a cup of coffee.

As he sat down, he heard the sound of laughter from next door. When he turned to look, he saw Molly heading toward him. Ben was sitting on the porch watching his daughter while still trying to give her a little space. Ben waved and Paul waved back.

Molly was holding the stuffed dog she always seemed to have with her. She had a smile on her face when she asked, "Is that coffee?" and pointed at his cup. Paul smiled back. "Yes, it is." Molly nodded a little and said, "Good." Then she sat down.

Paul looked up at Ben and shrugged. This was the first time Molly had ever sat down next to him. Ivy would color with her sometimes, and they had watched Molly a couple of times while

Marci ran to the store, but it had never been for more than an hour, and it was usually Ivy that Molly had interacted with.

She sat next to him and looked out around the neighborhood absently playing with the ear of her stuffed dog. He took another drink and just watched her for a minute. She seemed relaxed; he wondered if she was waiting for something. After a couple more sips, he asked, "What is the dog's name again?" trying to make conversation. Even though Molly appeared completely comfortable, just sitting and watching from the porch, Paul wasn't.

"Max," Molly replied.

Paul took another couple of sips. "I have your Jeep in my garage. Would you like me to get it?" he asked, almost getting up as he spoke.

Molly looked up at him. She had brown hair like her mother's, but it was back in a ponytail, and she had little freckles across her nose. Her brown eyes were soft when they met his gaze. "Are you done with your coffee?" she asked.

He looked down in the cup and had a little less than half of a cup left. He could have fibbed, but telling a four-year-old something that wasn't true seemed like a bad idea. "Not yet," he said.

"You should finish your coffee," she said and nodded again. It wasn't an order, but he wondered if all children were this insistent. He noticed she was looking around again at the movement up and down the street. Paul finally relaxed and finished his cup of coffee.

When he was done, he stood up, walked to the garage, and opened the door. As he did, Molly seemed to wait near the porch as if knowing she was in the right place for her dad to see her from his porch.

Paul brought the Jeep out. Molly simply said, "Thank you," got in, and drove back to her house. He waved as she drove away, grabbed his cup, and walked back into the house.

On Monday morning, Dr. Hayes asked how it was going. This was the question Paul was asked every Monday, and usually he said simply, "I'm okay. Seems a little better." However, this Monday, he told the doctor about Saturday morning and having his coffee with Molly on the porch. When Paul asked if this was normal for a four-year-old, the doctor only said, "Children are not always easy to predict. Sometimes they surprise us."

Paul immersed himself in work again for the week. On Saturday as he sat on the porch, he noticed Molly head over to sit with him again. She brought a juice box this time and seemed to drink it slowly. She didn't say anything for about 15 minutes. When Paul was almost done with his coffee, Ben strolled up and asked, "Would you like to come to dinner? We were going to do a cookout." Paul said yes and Molly got up, skipping back to her house. Paul watched her go with her father following behind.

He noticed that she had left her juice box on the porch. He picked it up and walked back into the house, not sure of what to make of what just happened.

He needed to get some groceries and drop off dry cleaning, so he showered and headed out. It was late in the afternoon when he returned home. He was bringing in bags when his phone rang. It was Marci.

"Hi. Paul?" she asked.

"Yes," he said.

"I was just checking to see if you were coming over for some BBQ? It would be nice of you to come by, and we have plenty of food." Marci's voice sounded uneven as if she weren't sure if she should be asking him.

"Yes, Ben asked. I would be happy to come by," he replied.

"Good then. We will see you at 6," she said, then hung up.

He put away his groceries and dry cleaning, did a several loads of laundry, and headed over next door right at 6. He had found a bottle of red wine in the cabinet above the fridge, and he brought it with him.

He was standing on the porch deciding if bowing out may be a better idea when the door suddenly swung open. It was Marci. "Hello, Paul," she said. He smiled. "Hello," he said back. Paul noticed Molly walk up behind Marci. "Ben's out back grilling," Marci said, gesturing for him to come in. He handed her the wine and thanked her again for inviting him.

It was then Molly who reached up and put her hand in his, tugging him toward the back door. Paul followed, careful not to squeeze her little hand to hard.

When they walked out back, Ben was at the grill, and it smelled amazing. "Hello," Paul said as Ben turned around, reaching out his hand. Paul reached out his hand to shake Ben's hand, letting go of Molly's. Ben smiled. "Marci was very happy to have you come over and join us," he said, turning back to the grill.

"I am happy to be here," Paul said, pretty sure he meant it.

"Would you like a beer?" Ben asked as Molly showed him where he would sit.

"Sure," Paul said, looking around for a beer.

Ben opened a small cooler near him and pulled out a bottle, passing it over. Paul took it, removed the cap, and took a swig.

"How is everything?" Ben asked. It took Paul a minute to realize that Ben wasn't using the same tone most did with him. Paul had started calling it the "I'm sorry" tone. The "I'm sorry" tone had an insidious way of almost pulling him into his grief again.

"Things are better," he honestly answered. He went on to tell Ben about the deal he had just closed. Ben told him about a new building he was working on that was being built downtown and supposed to be as "green" as a building could get.

They talked for about 20 minutes before Marci emerged carrying a salad from the kitchen. Paul started to stand, and she told him to sit, that she had it. She put the salad down and picked up a platter next to the grill for Ben to put the burgers and what looked like corn and potatoes. Paul watched them interacting and felt a small knot form in his stomach just as he felt a little hand on his arm. "Do you like veggies?" Molly asked. "I think they stink."

He looked over at her, and it made him smile. He turned back just as Marci brought the items over from the grill.

Paul tried to help, but he was politely shut down.

They ate and he enjoyed the company. They didn't once ask about Ivy. It was the first dinner out with people he knew other than for work where the topic of his wife wasn't brought up once. It was refreshing.

After dinner, Molly seemed to wander off and go color as Marci and Ben discussed their plans for the house, the weather, or the neighbors. It seemed like they were specifically avoiding topics that would upset him, and it made the night enjoyable. As it got later and Marci headed in to do dishes and put Molly to bed, he said, "I think I am going to get going. I want to thank you again for inviting me over."

Ben told him, "You are welcome anytime," and shook his hand. Since Ben was still putting up some of the items from dinner, Paul said he would show himself out. As he opened the door, Molly ran up and handed him a paper she had been working on. "For you," she whispered and looked in the direction of the kitchen before quietly sneaking back upstairs.

"Thanks," he said to Marci, then headed home.

When Paul got into his kitchen, he set down the paper on his counter. It was almost an exact copy of the last picture he had been given from Molly. It had a smiling yellow sun and a rainbow and said: "Bee Happy."

He grabbed his cup and moved for the bottle sitting on the counter, then paused. He set the cup back down and headed into the living room instead. Picking up the remote, he found a movie and settled in for the night.

On Monday in Dr. Hayes' office, Paul told him about his experiences on the weekend. The doctor was pleased to hear that there was social interaction outside of co-workers or clients. Paul told the doctor about the call he had received from Barbara and how she had asked about going through Ivy's things. Dr. Hayes asked him, "How do you feel about it?" Paul thought on it for a minute, then replied, "I don't think I am ready." The doctor seemed to contemplate this for a minute, then asked Paul, "Do you think you will ever be ready to say goodbye?"

Paul was a little stunned at the question and how it seemed to hit home. He hadn't thought about it much—saying goodbye. All he could say was "I don't think I am ready," but it was in almost a whisper.

Dr. Hayes tilted his head a little and said, "Her things are not her. Ivy is the memories you have of her and your life together. The stuff is just that: stuff. I am sure there are some sentimental items that you should hold onto; however, you cannot freeze time, Paul."

Paul could tell that the doctor was waiting for his words to sink in. When Paul finally looked up at him, the doctor simply said, "Wait until you are ready."

Paul called Barbara on Wednesday night. When she answered, he told her that she could come over on Saturday for lunch. Barbara thanked him and asked, "Is there was anything I can bring?"

Paul replied, "A few boxes."

Barbara paused for a moment, then said, "I can do that. See you Saturday."

Paul said, "See you then" and hung up the phone.

He closed his eyes and felt like he had been holding his breath for the entire phone call. He grabbed his cup, filled it, and walked into the living room.

On Saturday morning, he walked out to find Molly already sitting on the porch. She had her juice box, her stuffed dog Max, and a small plastic bag sitting next to her.

As Paul sat down, she smiled up at him and yelled, "Happy Saturday!" thrusting her arms in the air. He smiled and said, "Happy Saturday to you." She smiled back, picked up her juice box, and took a sip.

For several minutes, they sat in silence, watching the street. The sun caused the water from an early morning rain to glisten off the cars as it filtered through the leaves of the trees that lined the street. Paul turned to look at his small friend. She turned and met his gaze. "Me, Mom, and Daddy are going to the park today. What are you doing?"

"Well," he started, "I have lunch with my mother-in-law today." He tried to not sound sad.

"Sounds fun" was Molly's reply, not seeming to pick up on the feelings welling up inside of him. Paul knew it wouldn't be fun, that he didn't actually know if he could go through with it. But as Molly sat there regarding him, he realized she didn't understand the significance of the lunch or the weight of it. She was four, and it was as simple as he was having lunch with his family, and it should be fun.

When he finished his coffee and set the cup down, Molly stood up, grabbed Max and the bag that had been next to her, and thrust it out to Paul. "These are for you." Paul took the bag and opened it. Inside were two oatmeal cookies—his favorite. "Mom made them," she said and turned to head back to her house.

"Thank you, Molly," Paul shouted as she ran back to her father who sat on their porch, reading the paper.

He grabbed his cup and her empty juice box and headed inside with the cookies to prepare for lunch.

When Barbara pulled into the driveway, he felt the knot in his stomach again. He knew he wasn't ready, but Dr. Hayes' words sunk in. It didn't matter if he was ready; it wasn't about him. It was about Ivy.

Barbara greeted him with a hug which he returned. Paul had picked up some supplies for sandwiches for lunch. He didn't have an appetite, and it turned out that neither did Barbara.

He helped her grab some boxes she had left in her car. She told him she wasn't sure if he was really ready. "I didn't want to upset you," she said, tears welling in her eyes. He had to remember he wasn't the only one who lost someone. He hugged her again and began to build the boxes and tape the bottoms so that they were ready to be filled.

Barbara noticed the picture of the sun on his counter and held it up. "It's from Molly next door," he said. She smiled and put it on the fridge under a magnet from the local pizza delivery place.

"Where do you want to start?" Barbara asked.

"The closet," he said and grabbed several boxes, heading toward the bedroom. For the next few hours, Paul found himself on an internal roller coaster of emotions. Almost every item had a memory.

Barbara made sure that he knew that if there was anything he wanted to keep, he should just set it aside. He wanted to keep everything; instead, he kept a t-shirt from Ivy's college that she wore to bed during the winter. When he held it to his face, he could smell her. He walked into the other room and felt the tears.

Barbara came and sat with him, putting her arms around him. "That is enough for today," she said, pulling him close.

"Thank you," he said, nodding.

He helped her get the filled boxes to the car. When he returned inside, he saw the bag from Molly on the kitchen counter. He grabbed it and headed into his bedroom. He sat on the bed holding the shirt and eating the cookies. Ivy used to make the cookies for him as a surprise. He smiled when he remembered when he'd asked her why she didn't make them all the time, and her reply was "Because if you had them all the time, they wouldn't be a treat. A treat is a special thing for sometimes."

Ivy had been a treat.

On Sunday, he packed up more stuff himself. He went through her drawers and packed up her colorful sock collection. He packed away her yearbooks and mementos of her friends from school. He knew Barbara would know who to share them with. He found a shoe box in the top part of the closet. When he opened it, he found it was full of cards. They were cards he had given her. She had saved them. He closed the box and put it back on the shelf. He was done for today.

Dr. Hayes was very pleased with what Paul had accomplished. Paul also found himself a little proud that he was able to share that he had done what had seemed so far off just one week before. Dr. Hayes asked him what his next step was. Paul replied, "Keep going I guess." Dr. Hayes nodded.

The weeks got better. Molly was there each Saturday morning to have coffee with him. He found himself looking forward to these times and the simplicity of sitting with her. It had been a month since Barbara's first visit, and Paul had asked her to return to help him complete packing everything up.

At the end of the day, they had managed to pack up everything with the exception of the box of cards that sat atop the shelf in the bedroom. This was the last piece, but the one that he believed would prove to be the most difficult for him, and he decided to wait just one more week.

During the next session, Dr. Hayes asked him if he wanted to space out his sessions further. It was stated clearly that it was up to him, but the doctor felt that he was "in a better place." Paul thought about it and realized he was not crippled by his grief anymore. He agreed that he could spread out the appointments to once a month and that if any issues arose, he would call.

The week seemed to sail by, and on Saturday morning, he woke up to it raining. He opened the front door with the thought that he might see Molly sitting and waiting. She wasn't there. He was a little disappointed. He had gotten a couple of cupcakes for them to share. Since Molly had brought cookies once, it only seemed fair.

He decided to pull the box down from the shelf and bring it to the kitchen. He poured himself another cup of coffee and opened it.

The box seemed to contain every card or note he had ever sent Ivy. He had no idea she was saving them. The first one on top was from Valentine's Day. They had never given each other sappy romantic cards. This one had candy hearts, one of which had a bite out of it. On the inside it said, "Sweet as Candy," and he had signed it "Love You Always – PBJ." He set down the card on the counter. As he picked up and read every card, it was like traveling through some of the very best moments of their life together.

Although he'd begun to cry and that knot formed it his stomach, it became easier. He started to remember her smile more. He was most of the way through the box when he was reading a funny "Thinking of You" card he had given her "just because," and it hit him that Ivy, his Ivy, would be upset. She would be upset to think that he was in this state because of her. She would want him to celebrate her, to celebrate them. He smiled then, closing his eyes and imagining her chastising him.

He opened his eyes and picked up the last card in the box. It had a bee on the cover and when you opened it, the entire inside of the card was a smiling sun with a rainbow behind it. It said, "Bee Happy" in large letters and was signed "I want to always make you smile – PBJ." Paul looked up from the card to the fridge where Molly's picture was.

He grabbed the picture off the fridge and held them side by side. He put them on the counter and put all the other cards back into the box.

He looked to the window to find it had stopped raining. He looked back at the card and the picture on the counter. He grabbed the cupcakes off the counter and headed out the door.

He knocked on the door several times before Marci answered. "Is Molly here?" Paul asked. "I brought her some cupcakes." He held them out. Marci looked a little confused for a moment as she reached and took the package from Paul's outstretched hand. Shaking her head slightly, she said, "I'm sorry she isn't home. I will give them to her when she gets back. I am sure she will love them."

"When will she be home?" Paul blurted out. He sounded more aggressive then intended.

Marci took a half step back and said, "Paul, Molly is at her grandparents' house. She is there every Saturday."

"Every Saturday?" he asked.

"Yes, we take her there first thing in the morning and pick her up Sunday afternoon. Are you okay, Paul?" Marci asked.

"Yeah, thanks," he said as he turned to walk away.

When he got back to his house, he picked up the phone, staring at the card and picture. He dialed the phone. "Dr. Hayes? Yeah, this is Paul. I need to see you Monday."

JACOB

PART ONE: THE POLICY CHANGE

This had been one of the worst days in months in the ward. Brynn was at her wit's end. Nearing the end of a fourth twelve-hour shift, she had somehow instinctively ducked out of the way of a flying bed pan.

She looked up to see her assailant and found that it was Margaret. Brynn sighed and moved around the desk.

"Are you okay, Margaret?" Brynn didn't know why she was asking this question. She worked in the mental ward of one of the largest regional hospitals St. Michaels. Anyone who had been checked into this floor was less than okay.

Actually, this was true up until about two weeks ago. The management of the hospital had decided to change the strict admission policy that used to govern the ward. In the past, in order to be admitted to the Psych Unit, patients had to show signs at time of admission that they truly had a condition that needed treatment.

Doctors would evaluate patients before the admission paperwork even began and decide whether to admit. Although

Brynn had seen many flaws within this system, it had kept those who truly didn't need treatment out of her area of the hospital and spared her having to do the paperwork for every one of them.

As the Lead Charge Nurse, Brynn was responsible for all the other nurses and charts on her unit. It was a big misconception that nurses were run by the doctors. The nurses were almost an independent unit from the doctors with the exception of those functions that the nurse was not allowed to do, like write prescriptions or perform surgery.

When it came to keeping track of the patient's status, meds, and overall information, this task fell squarely to the nurses.

Because the hospital changed its policy to no empty beds, life was now a nightmare for all of the staff of Brynn's unit, doctors included.

The policy change was made by "upper management" in an attempt up the profits of the hospital. This of course didn't actually consider patient care. However, Brynn had found that in the business of healthcare, the bottom line had become more important than the actual people they cared for. Plus, because her unit at St. Michaels had followed the policy of only admitting those who needed care, they generally had empty beds. These beds would routinely get filled with the other area's castaways. Not because the patient didn't legitimately have a problem, but usually because they were a difficult case to manage.

Like Danny.

Danny was a manic who spoke constantly. This coupled with his need to be as offensive to those around him made him a horrible case for any hospital and would fray the nerves of even the most dedicated nurses.

Danny had been finally moved to the State Hospital two days ago. Although Brynn was happy to see him go, she knew that he would be more broken than he was now if he ever emerged again. There was a percentage that died on the inside.

The policy change applied to the entire hospital; however, the area that was feeling it the most was Psych. This understaffed area now attempted to handle patients without issues, getting in the way of caring for the patients who did—like Margaret who had suffered a breakdown after the death of her husband and been admitted after violent rages.

Margaret had actually been picked up and brought to the Unit after an incident at a grocery store that involved the destruction of several end cap displays. Looking at the frail and still visibly sad woman before her, Brynn couldn't fault her for being mad about her current lot in life. However, she could ensure the staff wasn't on the receiving end of the rage.

Brynn walked up to Margaret and asked, "What's wrong?" Brynn was prepared for anything including being punched in the face by this grandmother. It was even more heartbreaking when tears started streaming down her face uncontrollably.

Wrapping her arm around Margaret, Brynn turned and walked her toward her room, motioning to the med nurse for some Valium to help Margaret sleep. There wasn't a pill or shot in the world to take away the pain from losing a husband of over forty years.

Part Two: Filling a Bed

Brynn got Margaret settled just as she heard the one page she was hoping not to receive in the less than fifteen minutes before she was supposed to head out. There was a patient being brought up for admission. With no doctors currently on the unit, admission paperwork was required until he or she could be evaluated in the morning.

When Brynn got to the desk, there was a young man wearing scrubs sitting in one of the wheelchairs that the emergency room used to bring up intakes. He was accompanied by one of the interns who were usually relegated to the task of moving patients from unit to unit.

As she neared the two, the young man looked up and directly at her. His eyes were a piecing cobalt blue, and he looked at her face as if expecting something.

The intern cleared his throat which made Brynn realize she was staring at the young man in the wheelchair. The intern, she thought his name was Chris—they were never at the hospital long enough for it to matter or for her to care—handed her a folder and the clipboard, gesturing where she needed to sign, saying, "Turkey and Bed," nodding in the direction of the wheelchair.

"Turkey and Bed" usually meant a homeless person who was looking for a meal, shower, and warm and safe place to sleep. The name Turkey had come up because the cafeteria had a lot of days when a turkey sandwich was on the menu. Because he was wearing scrubs and holding a bag on his lap, she could almost confirm this to be the case.

She signed the receipt of the patient, Jacob Morrison, then handed the clipboard back to Chris or whatever his name was who quickly left the unit. Most interns disliked hanging around, and those who did usually were a little bit off in the head themselves.

Brynn opened the chart. This was not the first, fifth, or even tenth time Mr. Morrison had been seen by the doctors at St. Michaels. She reviewed the latest chart. He said he was seeing things that weren't there. This was a typical excuse used by the homeless to get them in for their brief stay. After the night passed, they would suddenly stop seeing things and quickly, because they had no form of payment, be released back into the world.

She looked up at him. "Do you know where you are, Mr. Morrison?"

"Jacob," he replied.

"What?" Brynn asked.

"Jacob. You can call me by my first name." He smiled.

Although he'd obviously been living on the streets for some time, he actually had a warm smile.

Brynn smiled back. "Okay then... Do you know where you are, Jacob?"

He held the smile and said, "I am in the Psych Unit of St. Michaels on the 8th floor. It is Thursday the fourth of October at about 10pm would be my guess."

Brynn nodded.

"Do you know why you are here?" she asked.

This was part of a series of questions to find out how lucid a patient was. Especially for those admitted at night, it was important to determine if they would need any form of sedation before they saw the doctor in the morning.

He looked down then, pursed his lips together, then spoke. "Yes. I am seeing things that aren't there. It has been happening the last couple of days." This was rehearsed. She had heard it hundreds of times.

"Can you walk?" she asked.

"Yes," he said, nodding.

"Okay then, let's get you a shower. I assume you remember the rules?" she asked.

Again he nodded and stood up from the chair. He was carrying a backpack along with what she assumed was the clothes he came in wearing. They make the patients take them off in the ER for fear of bedbugs or lice.

"I need you to give me your backpack which I will lock up until you check out, and I will make sure your clothes are washed tomorrow," she said, holding out her hand.

"Can I keep my book?" Jacob asked, handing over the bag of clothes first.

"Sure," she replied. He reached into the bag and pulled out a very worn copy of Cabal by Clive Barker, then handed her the backpack.

She gave him a puzzled look. "Are you sure that book is a good idea given the reason you're here?"

"It keeps me grounded," Jacob said, then headed for the showers.

Brynn took his backpack, noting the symbols all over it written in different pens and markers. She also tagged his laundry, put it in the bin, and had a tray of food brought in. When she was done, she saw Jacob emerge from the showering area.

"Are you hungry?" she asked, holding out the tray near the common room and indicating there was a table there he could sit at.

He smiled again. "Yes. Thank you."

He took the tray and went to eat.

Brynn placed him in a bed and turned over all the paperwork to her replacement for the night, Sarah. She checked in on him one more time before she left, making sure she introduced him and telling him that Sarah would help from there.

He smiled and looked at her a moment, studying her face, then nodded and returned to eating.

Part Three: Is this a health issue?

Brynn had managed to get a full six hours of sleep. She felt like this was a new record considering how the week had gone. She almost felt refreshed when she put on her scrubs, made a protein smoothie to take to work, and ate her oatmeal.

It was sometimes hard to maintain a healthy lifestyle with a high stress job with the only real option the food they serve in the cafeteria. Even the salads were questionable at best. Unless it was deep fried, Brynn wouldn't recommend putting it in anyone's mouth.

As she drove in, Brynn got a text from the overnight charge nurse.

[B– Marco is on your floor today. Wanted to warn you before you got here.]

Marco was the last person she needed assigned to her unit this week. He had been on the psych floor assigned to the unit for over four years. This was about three-and-a-half more than Brynn and most of the other nurses and techs believed he should have been.

Unfortunately, for all involved, Marco was under the delusion that he was the most amazing thing to exist on the floor and in the hospital in general. The last time he was assigned to Brynn's unit, he refused to listen to her as the lead, and when it came to doing the intake paperwork, he would suddenly need to be somewhere else. He angered the med nurse so badly that she had charged immediately into HR to file a formal complaint. Since Marco had been caught on camera, almost everyone believed that was the end of his reign on the floor. Apparently, that wish was just not intended to come true.

As the elevator doors opened, she heard the sounds of a struggle and screaming. When she got closer, she saw Marco and the med nurse Chris trying to restrain Jacob.

Jacob's eyes were locked on Marco, and he was screaming, almost begging him to let him go. Brynn dropped her stuff on the desk and headed to the med cart, and as she typed in her code, she asked, "What set him off?" She ended up repeating it twice, each time louder than the last.

"I went to check on him, and he just started freaking out," Marco said while Jacob struggled to break Marco's hold.

Brynn approached and yelled, "Jacob!" which for a brief moment seemed to snap Jacob out of the panic he was in. He was pale and sweating. Brynn could tell he was having a true attack, and he met her gaze and could only say, "Please help me... Please!"

Before Brynn could offer any soothing words, Marco said, "I will help you ... right back into your bed for the day!" He turned to Brynn and nodded while saying, "Do it!" Brynn hated sedating patients unless she had no other choice. This wasn't one of those situations.

"Jacob! Look at me!" Brynn knew she had only moments to retain any hope of controlling this situation. Jacob began to turn his head toward her again when Marco let go with one arm and grabbed the syringe Brynn had in her hand, removed the cap with his teeth, and jabbed it into Jacob's arm before she could react.

The look on Jacob's face was a terror that Brynn had rarely seen in a human. It was the look a person had when their abusive spouse or parent walked into the room.

The drug was fast acting, and Jacob began to slump in their arms. "What the hell was that?" Brynn asked Marco. "That was me handling the situation, which you seem incapable of doing." She rarely wanted to hurt another person; this was one of those moments. Brynn narrowed her eyes and was about to release on him when Chris said, "Let's get him cleaned up and into bed." Brynn looked down and saw that Jacob had soiled himself. Brynn looked from Marco to Chris, and she could tell from the look Chris was giving her she needed to do what he said.

As they brought him into his room, Marco let Jacob flop onto his bed and walked out. Brynn waited just a minute until she thought he was out of earshot to ask Chris, "What the hell happened?" as she began to peel off Jacob's clothes and clean him up.

"I don't know, B. Marcos arrived about an hour ago. We began to hand out the breakfast trays, and when Jacob came up to get his tray, he took one look at Marco, and his eyes filled with fear, like he knew him or he at least reminded him of someone he feared," Chris said as she continued to remove the dirty clothes and wipe Jacob down.

"Just looked at him and freaked out?" Brynn asked as he saw they had returned Jacob's clothes. She grabbed the bag, pulled out the articles of clothing, and began to redress him.

Chris nodded in reply, explaining: "Yes. However, as Jacob retreated, Marco followed him and eventually cornered him in the common room. When I got there, the screaming had already started, and Jacob was trying to get out and away from him. He kept saying something about monsters. He said Marco was a Reaper or something like that."

"Monsters?" Brynn asked, looking down at Jacob's tear-streaked face. "Has the doctor seen him yet?" She followed up before Chris answered the first question.

"No. Not yet," he said.

Brynn stood up. "Monsters," she whispered.

"What?" Chris asked.

"Nothing. Just wondering if this is medical," she said as she gathered the laundry and left the room.

"Are you thinking delusional?" Chris asked.

"It would explain the freak out. The doctor will have to decide for sure."

When Brynn got to the desk, she put her stuff away, grabbed Jacob's file, and set it on her desk. Hopefully, she had would have time later to review it. She grabbed the other charts and began the work that Marco should be doing right now. In this moment, she was almost thankful that he wasn't sitting next to her since she could feel her rage begin to boil again over what just happened.

When Dr. Hillman arrived a little after ten in the morning, Brynn had, much to her surprise, all the charts ready for review. She handed them one at a time as he reviewed them. Most he would just sign off on. When there was a proposed discharge or an intake, there was more work for them.

Mostly, the nurses made recommendations, while the doctors signed off. When Dr. Hillman got to Jacob's file, he paused. He flipped through some of the last charts within the file, then looked at Brynn. "Drug case?"

Brynn shrugged, saying, "I don't know. He seemed very coherent last night. If it is spice though, there would be no way to know."

The doctor nodded, made a note, then said, "Order a CBC and a tox screen." He handed the folder back.

The thought of asking Dr. Hillman if he was interested in seeing the patient first before ordering any tests was ridiculous. Most of the time, the doctors treated the patients by the doctor's opinion of what they thought was wrong with the person.

Unfortunately, most mental conditions a person can suffer from were a combination of symptoms and instead of being able to actually test for what the patient was suffering from, they had to test for all the other things it can be and eliminate them. For instance, when someone is schizophrenic, they test to see if the patients had syphilis. If they didn't, then they could actually have a mental disorder.

If a doctor was unwilling to take the time and figure out if the person they were talking to was on drugs, had a medical condition, or was just suffering from a chemical or hormone imbalance, then they simply ended up in an endless cycle of possibly not being treated for what was actually wrong with them. This unit didn't take that time.

Brynn took the folder and smiled the practiced smile of a nurse. "I will let you know as soon as the results are in." Since he was done with all the patient files, Dr. Hillman headed for the doctor's lounge on the third floor.

Taking blood from Jacob was easy. He was still out and therefore could not consent. Not that they needed his consent, but having the veil of patient rights sometimes were worth the work.

The results were negative. When Brynn relayed this news to Dr. Hillman, she had to remind him who Jacob was and the reason he had ordered the tests. The result was Jacob being labeled delusional and prescribed injections of Haldol, Ativan, and Benadryl. The injection needles were huge and painful. He would be knocked out for hours. This also meant that he was staying. It was considered harmful to society to have someone who wasn't on proper medication roaming the streets. So until his illness was under control, he was now a resident.

He was also considered a goldmine as a patient. Most of the time those that see things that weren't really there only did for a very short period of time or had no touch with reality. Jacob had both which made for a challenge in the mental health industry.

PART FOUR: NO REAL CHOICE

When Jacob woke up that night, he was given a late dinner. Although he had an IV while he was out, it never made up for real food. As he finished up the second pudding, Brynn walked in to check on him one more time before she left for the night.

When she came in the room, he didn't look at her before he said, "When can I leave?" His voice held a hint of anger.

Brynn walked closer to him. "I am not sure, Jacob..." She waited to see if he would turn around. "We just want to make sure you are okay. That's why you came here, isn't it?"

His head fell a little before he said, "I came here for food and a fucking shower. We both know that." He raised his head and turned to look at her. "I want to leave. You can't keep me here."

This was one of the parts she hated most about her job, the part where she took away the patient's right to choose. She realized that most could actually make choices about their care, but the state felt that it knew best. The hospital could hold a person for a minimum of 72 hours without their permission. It was called the Baker Act. Then if they proved they needed that extended, there was an attorney appointed to their case, and it would go before a judge.

"Jacob, you had a pretty bad incident today. Dr. Hillman feels it would be best..."

She was cut off. "Dr. Hillman didn't even talk to me. Dr. Hillman is keeping me drugged to the point of a coma. Dr. Hillman isn't here." Jacob was getting worked up. His face had flushed as he stood up and shouted, "LET ME GO!"

Brynn began to move toward him using the most calming voice she could. "Jacob, it is just for..." He picked up his tray and threw it at her before almost stumbling. The drugs were still in his system. "You," he looked her in the eyes again, "can't stop me." He headed for the door just a Chris the med nurse came around the corner. Brynn could tell he had more meds on him.

When Jacob saw Chris in the doorway, he paused for a moment. It seemed he was ready to attempt to storm out with only Brynn to stop him. The suddenly he began running. He pushed right past Chris and Brynn moved to hit the alert button.

As Jacob took off down the hall, Brynn called for a Code Grey. This meant that the psych unit had a runner. All of security, the other unit, and most of the male nurses came to the call. Within moments, Jacob was restrained and getting another dose of his drug cocktail. It should keep him out the rest of that night.

Sarah, the charge nurse taking over for Brynn, offered to do the report. It would be about an hour of paperwork, and Brynn was working on her eleventh hour of being on the clock. Her nerves were frayed, and she knew she needed to get something to eat and take a break. Brynn thanked Sarah, grabbed Jacob's file, and headed out.

Part Five: Monsters are Real

Brynn had called for take-out on her way home. It kept her from eating junk food and made it so she didn't have to cook. She got home and took a long hot shower. She poured herself a glass of wine and ate her dinner while watching some mindless sitcom. This was her nightly ritual to simply unwind.

She cleared away the to-go boxes, poured herself another glass of wine, and pulled Jacob's file from her bag.

She returned to the beginning when Jacob was eighteen. It appeared he had records from before he turned eighteen, but his childhood records were sealed. There was a notice that she could request them from the State. That meant he had been in the foster system. Most children who ended up with a mental disorder and were in the foster system stayed there.

His records indicated that he came in every couple of months. He usually was only in for the night and then released. She could tell that he was one of those people who could work the system. He would always claim something that was easily treatable with a prescription which Brynn was sure he would fill and sell on the streets.

As she flipped through chart after chart of when he was brought in, it all began to blend together up until an incident about six months ago. He came into the ER again complaining he was depressed. There was a new intern on staff that night, Nathan Montgomery. She remembered him because he always made her uncomfortable when he brought someone up to the unit.

The file indicated that Jacob had a reaction when Nathan came in the room to do the initial exam. Jacob wouldn't respond to questions, and when Nathan called for help, Jacob pushed his way out of the room and ran out of the ER. This visit was the first time he had returned since.

Brynn knew there had to be something more to this. A person wasn't usually as sane and stable as Jacob appeared to be, then suddenly have a violent reaction to a particular person. Jacob had a problem with Marco and Nathan specifically. They didn't look anything like each other.

Brynn sighed and put the file down. Polishing off the last bit of wine, she wished she were heading to a huge bed covered in fluffy pillows and satin sheets where she could sleep as long as she wanted. Instead, it was a full-size bed with cotton sheets she hadn't had a chance to wash in weeks, and she had to be up again in six hours. Not the life she dreamed of.

As she was falling asleep, she remembered something Chris had mentioned that Jacob had said just before he had been sedated. He said that Marco was a Reaper. It was a very specific statement. Usually when people saw monsters, they saw them everywhere; it didn't add up.

Her phone went off, and she thought it was her alarm. After trying to turn the alarm off and realizing it wasn't going off, she answered the phone, catching it on the last ring. "Hello?"

"Brynn, it's Chris," his voice was strained, "I need you to come in... Now!"

It took her a moment. "What's happening?" There was a pause. "Chris?" Brynn asked, feeling some panic. Chris finally continued, but his voice was almost a whisper. He was speaking fast. "Marco is here and is waking up the patient. Says he needs to talk with him before the doctor gets in. Get here... Now!" Then he hung up.

Brynn looked at the time, 2 am, sighed, got out of bed, and began to get ready. She didn't bother with her normal morning ritual or smoothie preparation. She simply grabbed her bag, keys, and headed out the door. Chris didn't tell her which patient because she already knew.

When she exited the elevator, there was a huge commotion around the room Jacob had been staying in. There was security pounding on door. As she approached the door, Chris came up and filled her in. "Marco decided to speak to him alone. He went in and locked the door. That was fifteen minutes ago. I heard laughter, then yelling, more like screaming. Then, silence."

Brynn looked at the officers. "Break it down," she said, leaving no doubt that they were to do as she commanded. One of the guards nodded to the other and readied to do her request when the door opened.

Marco walked out, his arms covered in what looked like scratches and blood. Brynn pushed past the guards and headed into the room. "What the hell do you think you're doing?" she directed toward Marco.

When she got into the room, Jacob was on the floor. He had bruises and scratches and a wound on his head. She kneeled and took his pulse. He was bleeding and his pulse was weak, but he was still alive. "Chris!" she hollered, looking at his wounds.

When Chris entered, they helped get Jacob onto the bed. Chris had brought a kit with him. "I got this. Go deal with that," he said, gesturing to the door. Brynn looked down at Jacob one last time, then nodded to Chris and headed out. Security was still waiting outside, and she pointed at Marco who was standing at the charge nurse desk. "Have him escorted to ER to check his injuries and then I want a report filed."

Marco looked back at her, and a smile crept across his face, then Brynn swore that she saw something in his eyes—a darkness that sent chills down her spine.

The security guards approached him, and he put his hands up. "I'll go willingly." He turned to look at Brynn, and in a voice that attempted to sound sultry, he added, "This isn't over." He winked and headed in the direction the guards were leading.

When he was through the first double doors, she went to check on Jacob.

Chris had him mostly bandaged and back in bed. "I think he injected him with insulin." Brynn sighed. "What was Marco doing here? What are you doing here?" Chris shook his head and started putting the kit away. "I got a call from Trina. She told me she and the med nurse, Mike, both got sick and had to leave. They started the call around and got a hold of me and Marco." Chris stood up. "It was really crazy, and I dunno, Marco is a dick, but I have never seen something like that. He just lost it."

Brynn helped finish the clean up of the room and checked on Jacob one more time. He seemed stable but would need some further tests when the doctor got in to make sure.

She then took a little time to ensure the rest of the floor was okay. Chris took on the duties of the charge nurse while she did the meds and helped with charting. She saved Jacob's for last, and as she updated with the information she knew and Chris provided, she flipped through to see if Marco was anywhere in his records. He wasn't.

It was now four in the morning. Chris had gone to get some coffee and a snack for both of them, promising it would be something that arrived at the hospital pre-wrapped and wasn't made in the cafeteria. Neither of them wanted to take any chances that whatever had gotten the other nurses sick wasn't the featured meal of the night.

As she was sitting flipping through Jacob's file again, Brynn decided to do something that was not normally a great idea. She went to the patient lockers and pulled out the backpack and now clean clothes Jacob came with.

He had arrived wearing a shirt that said, "Succulent Apothecary" which Brynn assumed was a band or a head shop somewhere. He had ripped jeans, socks, sneakers, and a hoodie that had symbols drawn all over it in different inks.

She then looked at the backpack with the matching symbols. She turned to look around to see if there was anyone around. She knew she would hear Chris when he opened the doors at the end of the hall. There were cameras almost everywhere, but the only time they seem to be monitored was when someone was going back to check footage.

In the backpack, she found more clothes. They were dirty so she pulled them out and put them in another laundry bag to be cleaned. The other things she saw were soap in a bag, toothbrush, toothpaste, comb, old cell phone, a wallet that only held an expired ID, a folded photo of a family, and two books that looked like journals.

Brynn pulled out the first one and found more of the symbols. Just then she heard the sound of the door being opened. She put the book aside, loaded the backpack into the locker, grabbed the bag of clothes and book, and headed back out.

She dropped the bag to be cleaned in the laundry pick up after filling out the slip, and Chris looked at her, questioning. "Found it sitting out in the other room. They must have forgotten to wrap it up." She didn't know why she was lying. Chris she could trust, he wouldn't care, but for some reason she cared.

They sat drinking the coffee and eating the powdered doughnuts and mini chocolate chip cookies he had found. Normally, this wouldn't be her choice, but the warm coffee and sugar provided a kind of comfort.

Chris got up to make a round to check on everyone. This would take a few minutes, so Brynn pulled out the book. It was a diary of sorts. It had some dates and notes, but also a lot of sketches of horrible creatures. As she flipped through the pages, she noticed the notes were descriptions of when and where Jacob had seen these monsters.

There was more detail than Brynn would have imagined in something other than a Stephen King novel. Some of them had names while others had the description of how they smelled and how Jacob felt when he saw them. It also listed how many times Jacob had seen the creatures.

Brynn pulled out his chart and looked for the date of the emergency room visit where he had run out. She found it and compared it to the journal. She was shocked at what she read. The creature didn't have a name, but it had a large bulbous head with an elongated jaw. He had drawn at least three rows of teeth and spittle dripping down the front of the almost skeletal frame. Long claws protruded from its three fingers, and it had what looked like eyestalks in its shoulders.

The image was so real even though only a sketch. If she closed her eyes, she could imagine this thing was there, looking at her as if she were a succulent morsel it wanted to rip apart and eat. Brynn shivered.

She closed the book and knew that for Jacob the monsters were real.

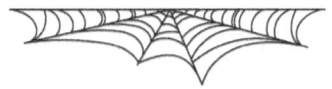

Part Six: The Reaper

Brynn had been scheduled on the morning shift with another two nurses. Chris actually had the day off so when the other two arrived, Brynn told him he could go even though he tried to talk her into letting him take her place. She knew how valuable time off could be to people in this line of work. If he let himself get too fried, he would be useless to anyone.

Brynn had done the morning rounds somewhat on auto-pilot. When the breakfast arrived, she handed out the Styrofoam trays and spoons. These were least likely to cause harm to others, plus they did a spoon count at every meal to ensure the some-what dangerous weapons were returned. She was surprised when Jacob got in line.

She was reaching for the next tray when his eyes met hers. Jacob's eyes were a darker blue then she remembered. He had dark circles underneath, and they were rimmed with red.

As he reached for the tray, there was a sorrow in his gaze. It was the kind of look she saw sometimes in patients who decided they were trapped, like animals in a cage when all the fight has gone out of them.

Brynn had thought she was numb to it, that look. In this moment, she felt the same feeling of sadness as the first time she had seen that look on patient's face when she had started years ago. Whatever wall she had erected to hold that back was shattered in this one moment.

She handed Jacob the tray, and he let his lips form a small smile and he said, "Thank you." All she could do was nod. Brynn pursed her lips. She knew she was tired and that although she had worked double before, somehow this was too much, and she felt tears stinging her eyes. She finished handing out the trays to the remaining people in line, then rushed to the bathroom.

She went into a bathroom in an empty patient room. She placed her hands on the sink and let her head hang for a moment and just breathed. What the hell is wrong with me? She had grown fond of some of her patients before. Most of them were good people, and she had empathy as most had a very traumatic life or life event that brought them here.

She turned on the water and splashed it on her face. The cool feeling let her calm a little. She splashed it one more time and turned off the water, grabbing several paper towels, then used them to dry her face.

She threw them in the trash bin and turned to make sure she didn't look terrible. The moment her eyes hit the mirror she saw Marco or what she thought was Marco—but his eyes were completely black, and he had spiked ridges down his forehead. He opened his mouth and a forked tongue snaked out toward her. Brynn jumped and spun to defend herself to find no one behind her.

When she looked into the mirror again, she was the only face she saw. She looked around again and back to her reflection, then moved out of the bathroom, shutting off the light.

I'm losing it, she thought. Normally, a person in her position would say she was going crazy. She was seeing things that weren't there, and those things were the stuff of nightmares. Knowing she lacked sleep, she could chalk it up to simply imagining things. Some part of her hoped that was the case and she was simply nearing the end of her rope stress wise. That would mean a couple days off and rest would fix it. Seemed simple enough.

As she returned to the desk, she grabbed the journal and flipped through the pages until she found what she searched for: The Reaper.

Her eyes were glued to the page. The eyes were black, the head had ridges all over it that matched the ones she had seen on Marco in the bathroom, and the tongue was long and forked. How could she have imagined exactly what was drawn here? Had she seen the page earlier that night and some part of her subconscious recreated it? The rational part of her started trying to explain it. She had to explain it.

Just then, Dr. Hillman walked up. "Whatcha reading?" he asked. Brynn jumped, having been so wrapped up in her own thoughts his voice startled her. She looked up at him, then grabbed a pencil to mark the page and put the book down "Just an old journal," she said, faking a smile. "Anything juicy in there?" he chuckled. She knew he was just trying to make her smile, but he had picked the wrong morning. "Only if you're a thirteen-year-old girl," she replied, again faking a smile and a little laugh.

Dr. Hillman went through all the files and chose four he said he wanted to meet with. Jacob was one of them. He also made sure to order several more blood and urine tests for him based on the incident that happened that morning.

When he handed her the order for the tests, he said, "Heard about Marco. Was it as crazy as they say?" Brynn didn't know how to answer that. It seemed like there wasn't a safe answer to it. She knew what Marco did was wrong. If they found he had given Jacob anything that the doctor hadn't prescribed, his career was over. What she couldn't understand was why Marco would risk it. There was no way this young man was worth that to him, or was he? Brynn looked at the doctor. "It was very weird. Not sure if Marco just needs a break." Dr. Hillman nodded, grabbed his coffee, and headed to the treatment office where he could meet with the patients one-on-one. Brynn thought then to call down to find out what had happened with Marco.

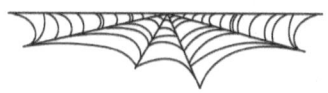

PART SEVEN: YOU ARE NEVER ALONE

Brynn called and was placed on hold for what seemed like hours. It was most likely fifteen minutes, but the fact of the matter was lack of sleep, the craziness that happened last night, and seeing monsters herself had caused an almost collapse of whatever shreds of consciousness she had left.

"Hello?" asked a voice on the other end of the phone. "Who are you holding for?" They sounded slightly annoyed; Brynn didn't care.

"I was waiting to hear the status of a nurse brought into the ER by security several hours ago: Marco Ramirez." Brynn had no hope of suppressing the annoyance of asking the same thing for the fourth time this call.

She heard shuffling papers, then, "Says here he never finished the intake paperwork."

Brynn said, "What?" knowing the answer was the same.

"Didn't finish paperwork. Listen, we are slammed down here, so if there is nothing else?"

Brynn shook her head and realized the person couldn't see her. "No... thank you," she said, hanging up the phone.

The next call she made was to security. The guard who answered the phone explained Marco went to the bathroom and never came back. Since there were no bathrooms in the ER rooms, they let him go to a general one, and after thirty minutes of him not coming out, they went in, and he was gone. The guard continued to talk, but the receiver fell into Brynn's lap, and her hands went to her face. Only when Dr. Hillman tapped her on the shoulder did she finally notice the phone. "You okay?" he asked; there was genuine concern in his voice.

Brynn hung up the phone. "Yes, I am fine. Just tired." She looked up and applied the fake smile or as close as she could come to it.

Dr. Hillman narrowed his eyes. "Do you need something?" He was intimating that he would write her a prescription. This seemed like a nice gesture; however, it always bothered Brynn how easy it was for some doctors to be willing to "be nice" until they needed something in return.

"No. Thank you. Just need an actual night's sleep."

He laughed a little at that. Brynn debated telling him about Marco and how he had run. She didn't know that Dr. Hillman would do anything but comment on the issue and try to comfort her. She didn't need comforting.

She reached for the folders he held. "Anything I need to note?" She was back in job mode.

"No. All good." He smiled.

Normally she would have taken the comment and just put the paperwork away, but she didn't understand. "Do I need to file anything on the situation with Marco?"

Dr. Hillman shook his head. "Mr. Morrison doesn't remember anything from last night. My guess is whatever caused the issue was because of a reaction to the drugs he was on."

It took every little bit of strength Brynn had left to not lunge over the workstation and punch Dr. Clueless in the face. Instead, she smiled and said, "That must be it." That confirmed he would be no help with Jacob or Marco.

Dr. Hillman grabbed his coffee again and headed for the doctor's lounge while Brynn set to work on the charts, again saving Jacob's for last. She didn't understand. Did he really not remember the attack?

She read through the very sparse notes that the doctor had made. Nothing.

Brynn grabbed the journal, slid it into her bag, and let the charge nurse on duty know she was heading out. She was going to be useless if she continued to stay. She walked past the common room and saw Jacob sitting there reading his book.

With what he saw, she could not imagine how it was calming.

When Brynn got home, she took a long hot shower. She needed to calm the thoughts racing through her mind. When she got out of the shower, she normally used a towel to wipe the steam away. Tonight, she left it there. She told herself she just didn't care, but deep down, she knew she was scared of what or more specifically who she would see.

PART EIGHT: NO TRUTH

Brynn had been lying in bed for about an hour when she decided she could no longer deny that she couldn't fall asleep. Normally with a day like this, sleep came easy but not tonight. She got up and made herself some chamomile tea, and as she waited for the water to boil, she noticed Jacob's journals poking out of the top of her bag.

Part of her knew opening it was a bad idea. However, she was trained as a nurse. She had heard patients describe their delusions before. She actually used to love to listen and watch them in their own worlds. She didn't want to be in Jacob's world.

She started with the first page. It was Jacob describing the reason for the journal:

> *I know that I am different now. I haven't met anyone else that sees them, the monsters. The first one I saw was when I was ten. It was a substitute math teacher. Looking back now and knowing what I know, I did everything wrong. It knew I could see it, and it followed me home. My parents... I would say they protected me. They did this by dying. I was saved by running.*

I could explain my story, but all that you need to know is I never let a family like me. This way I wouldn't stay. Only long enough to be fed, change of clothes. If I saw one I thought may start to accept me, I knew I had to leave. I started carrying everything I needed with me. I could never lead them to people again.

I found the symbols in the days I spent in libraries. They mean protection in many different languages and cultures. However, I have never found anything about the monsters themselves.

I sometimes see in video games and comics creatures that look similar. I think they are from a dark part of our pasts that have been buried, and no one wants to dig them up.

I am now eighteen. I am free of the system, for now at least. The only thing I can do at this point is make sure I can never get trapped. The last one almost ended my life. If you are reading this, I might be dead. I hope I am dead and not trapped by one. I would rather die quickly.

It made more sense now. As she thumbed through the pages, they described each encounter, where and when, and it seemed every detail Jacob could remember.

The journal indicated that Jacob moved around a lot. Every time he encountered one of these creatures, he would attempt to get at least twenty miles away. He thought that seemed to be the distance where they, the creatures, could no longer find him.

He described in detail how he almost lost his life in the beginning by not knowing the creatures could track and follow him once he was discovered.

Jacob had researched everywhere he could think of, but he didn't know how the creatures knew he could see them for what they really were. He also didn't have any idea what he looked like to them.

She came across the page again with the Reaper. This was one of the creatures that Jacob had almost lost his life to. Chills ran down Brynn's spine when she remembered the mirror and the look in Marco's eyes when he walked away from her.

Then, it suddenly occurred to her: Marco knew she could see him.

Part Nine: Trapped

Brynn threw on a pair of jeans, shirt, hoodie, and sneakers. She grabbed the journal and her bag and raced back to the hospital. The entire drive, her mind was almost fighting. There was a large part, the rational part, that knew this couldn't possibly be real. That she was having some kind of breakdown, and this was a result. There were cases of shared delusions, and although rare, it would explain everything.

All her training, everything she knew, told her this was the case. However, a small part of her, the part that crept in right as she was falling asleep, the part that made her hold out hope that those things she could imagine were real was telling her that what Jacob and what she was now seeing was real.

She quickly parked her car, grabbed her bag and badges, and ran up the stairs to the unit. She got through the door, and Chris was behind the desk. "I thought you were off tonight?" he asked, looking startled to see her. She must look almost frantic.

Then it occurred to her she didn't know what to say or how to say it. Why would she need to talk to a patient, let alone in the middle of the night?

"Are you okay?" Chris asked.

She could tell he had already assumed she wasn't. "I... umm... I..." She was fumbling. "I am... I forgot ... something." She walked into the storage room and got Jacob's back pack and his clothes. She took a breath and tried to come up with what she was going to say. She walked out and started with, "Chris, I know this will sound..." She couldn't even finish the sentence before she felt the chill go up her spine. Turning, she saw Marco enter through the hallway doors.

Brynn didn't see actually see the Marco she knew. She saw the Reaper in all of its gory details. She was paralyzed. The claws were dripping, barbed tail moving from side to side, maw grinning as if a cat playing with its prey. Brynn couldn't even breathe; she had never been this terrified in her life.

"Marco, you can't be here. I am calling security," Chris said loudly. Only this broke the trance, and Brynn used this moment to turn and run toward Jacob's room. She didn't look back for fear she would not be able to move again. There was still commotion happening behind her, and as she opened the door, she dared to glance back to see the Reaper swinging at Chris.

She closed the door when she got inside, but there were no locks. She moved over to Jacob's bed with only a little light from under the door to guide her.

"Jacob?" she whispered. "Jacob. Wake up... Please." She knew she sounded desperate, but she also knew she didn't have a lot of time. Even though Chris was larger in stature than Marco, Chris didn't know what he was actually fighting.

"What?" she heard Jacob say.

Brynn loosed a little sigh of relief. She had feared he was already dead. "Jacob, it is Brynn. Your nurse. We have to go.

Marco, I mean, the Reaper is back." She grabbed his clothes and handed them in his direction. When she felt his hand touch hers, there was a warm tingle. She tried as she let the clothes go to remember if she had actually touched him before. She couldn't remember.

She stood up and went to listen at the door. As she looked away to give Jacob some privacy to change, she tried to strain to hear what was going on with the altercation. She didn't hear anything. She slowly opened the door to look.

She had to put her hand over her mouth not to scream at the vision before her. The Reaper was standing atop the limp and bloodied body of Chris, pulling out entrails from his abdominal cavity and eating them.

She was about to turn when she felt the same warm tingle against her back. Jacob's voice whispered in her ear, "We have to go… Now!"

He grabbed her hand and slowly opened the door, gesturing for her to be quiet. He started to look to see what direction they should head. Brynn knew that the only exit without raising alarms was past the creature. She pointed down the other hall. It would set off an alarm and a lock down that she would figure out how to get past once they had a head start.

She pulled his hand and began to move. They got to almost the end of the hall when she heard the growl and roar come from behind them. It had seen them. She swiped her badge and pushed on the door. Without the badge, it would take ten seconds for the door to open, and they didn't have that time.

Once she cleared the door, she began to run down the stairs. The alarm was sounding, and there were seven floors and fourteen flights. She knew they had to stop on the second or third as security would be waiting at the first.

Trusting Jacob was still behind her, she kept moving.

They were down about four flights when something crashed into the door above. They had ten more seconds, and she didn't trust herself to look up and not lose all of them. She kept moving.

At seven flights down, the door burst open. She heard the roar again. It sounded more aggressive. It was moving and fast. When she got to the next landing, she pushed the door open and again hoped Jacob was following.

She looked around, trying to get her bearings as to what floor she was on. Pediatrics? Shit! She thought and took off in a random direction. She could only think that she hoped it didn't hurt the kids here.

Most of the floors had similar layouts; she just needed to find another stairwell. Just as they reached the door, there was a scream behind them. Brynn turned to see that the creature had a woman, a nurse, by the throat and was holding her up.

Jacob grabbed her arm. "We have to go," he said as he pulled her through the door. Without letting go, he flew down the stairs, pulling Brynn along. As they moved to the second floor, Brynn stopped. "We have to exit here." Jacob pulled open the door and moved her to go through first. He removed his hospital bracelets then and dropped them inside the stairs. They heard a familiar crashing from above. It was in the stairwell.

The second floor was the main floor of the hospital which held radiology, pharmacy, and most of the administrative offices. Most were closed now. Brynn moved quickly and toward the staff only area. This had an exit to the parking garage. The alarms continued to blare as they moved, only changing course as a few security guards headed toward another hallway. They were doing their sweeps.

After that slight delay, they wound through several corridors to the door they needed and exited to the garage. Brynn ran to her car, unlocked it for both of them, and told Jacob to get in the back seat. Her windows were fairly well tinted back there, and she didn't think they could both leave.

As she drove out of the garage, she was stopped but only for a second as she showed her ID and was allowed to pass. They are really too trusting, she thought as she sped away.

She kept checking her rearview mirror, thinking at any moment it would be behind her. After she had driven several blocks, Jacob said, "It is not that fast." She was startled as she had been so wrapped up in making sure she didn't drive off the road and trying to calm her burning lungs, she had all but forgotten he was back there.

"What?" she asked, her throat dry from running.

Jacob sat up and looked forward, meeting her gaze in the rearview mirror. "They are not that fast. It will chase us, but it will take some time to catch up." She almost didn't hear what he said. His eyes, his face, his lips—they had all changed. There was almost a glow to them.

Suddenly, she heard a horn and realized she had drifted out of her lane. She righted the car and decided to keep her eyes on the road. "I live about fifteen minutes from here. We can go there."

She assumed Jacob nodded because he didn't say anything else, and they drove in silence for the rest of the ride.

Part Ten: Choices

When Brynn pulled up to her house, she got out of the car and walked up to the door. She heard the other car door, and as she turned the key, she felt Jacob behind her. She opened the door and went into the house. She went to the kitchen first, throwing her bag on the counter and opening the cabinet to get some glasses before filling them at the fridge.

She turned to hand Jacob a glass and saw he was looking at his journal that had spilled out of her bag.

"Did you read this?" he asked without facing her.

"Yes," she replied.

He opened it and seemed to be looking randomly at the pages before turning to meet her gaze.

Brynn marveled. She had never seen anything like what she was looking at. Jacob took the glass from her outstretched hands. "What did you see?"

She blinked, then swallowed another sip of water as if this might change what was before her now. Licking her lips, she then said, "You are glowing."

Jacob furrowed his eyebrows. "Glowing?" he asked. His voice had an intensity now that was causing a reaction Brynn wasn't sure she could explain.

She nodded and continued, "Your skin has a light glow beneath the surface as if you saw a light under ice."

Jacob smiled. "What else?" he urged her.

"Your eyes have a crystalline quality. They are blue, but sapphire blue, and they look like a gemstone." She paused for a moment, then continued, "Your features are more angular than they were before, and there are tiny lines that crisscross your skin. I didn't see them at first, but in this light as you move, they are there."

Jacob turned and picked up his journal, grabbed a pen from her bag, and began to draw something. It only took him a few moments, then he turned to show her what was on the pages. "Like this?" he asked.

The sketch, although using black ink, captured what she described. She smiled. "You are pretty good at that."

He returned the smile. "Thanks. It has been a useful skill."

Brynn didn't know what else to say standing in the kitchen with a perfect stranger. A very alluring perfect stranger. She closed her eyes, took a long deep breath, and opened them again.

"Are we far enough?" she asked.

Jacob looked around as if trying to sense something. "I think so. Does he know where you live?" he asked.

"No." She shook her head. "He shouldn't." But Jacob didn't seem convinced.

"We should go somewhere else," he finally said. Brynn at first wanted to think he was asking her. He wasn't. She nodded, put the glass down, and went to her bedroom to grab a couple things. Then to the bathroom for a toothbrush. As she did these trivial tasks, she decided to focus only on what needed to happen next.

Too many thoughts pulling at her would cause her to waver and even though this was her house, she wasn't safe. When she had gathered everything, she found Jacob waiting at the door with his backpack in hand.

"We don't have to go together. It is dangerous... You know... I'm dangerous." He wasn't meeting her gaze. He was right. He was dangerous.

It took only a moment for her to grab his hand and say, "I know."

Nothing else needed to be said. They got in the car and drove for another few hours until they decided to stop at a motel that was just off the highway. Brynn checked in for them. She paid in cash, but they asked for ID so they had her real name. She figured this was pretty safe because Marco or whatever Marco was would have to call every motel for miles and miles to find them.

They got to the room. It had two queen beds. Brynn went to the bathroom since they had been on the road a while, and she also needed a moment alone. She was exhausted. She had a million questions she needed to ask him but knew that it could wait. She finished up, washed her hands, and shut off the light.

When she entered the room, Jacob stood up from the edge of the bed and walked up to her. Before she knew it, he had wrapped his arms around her, and she was in the most comforting and stimulating hug she had ever had. She closed her eyes and just breathed him in.

For the first time in days, she felt at peace.

After a couple minutes Jacob whispered, "Thank you."

Her instinct almost took over and she was going to ask, "For what?" But she knew.

She had saved his life tonight. Then she felt a stabbing pain remembering Chris and the other nurse, and she had no idea who else had died tonight because of this. They were just in its way to get to Jacob. Why had he been worth more than them? Jacob pulled back and looked down at her. His thumb wiped the tears streaming down her face. She wanted him to say something, anything, that would make what happened okay. He wouldn't... couldn't. Because nothing could make a loss like this okay. Jacob had lost his parents to one of these things. He knew the cost and the pain it brought.

He pulled her close again for a moment, then whispered, "You should sleep." He backed up, moving toward one of the beds, and pulled the covers aside. She sat down on the now exposed sheets, and he kneeled to unlace her sneakers, pulling each one off and setting it aside. He helped remove her hoodie, then she laid back in the bed as he covered her with the blankets.

He looked down at her and smiled slightly then bent farther and kissed her forehead. "I will be right here," he said. She smiled back and rolled to the side, letting herself fall into darkness.

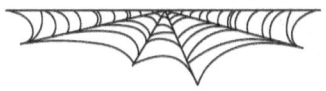

Part Eleven: Endings

Jacob had watched her fall asleep knowing the burden she now had. When she had described how he looked to her, he didn't know if he should explain he was seeing the same thing in her face. His drawing was based on how she appeared to him, not just the words she said.

He knew this would be too much for her. He didn't know what she or he now were, but he knew that this was all new to him. Jacob had been alone for a long time. He had friends from time to time but none of them really knew until Brynn.

He watched her sleep for a while, then used the restroom and got into the other bed. He wanted to be next to her, to feel what he felt only when he touched her, but he again needed to give her time. She had just unknowingly given up her whole life because she couldn't go back.

Jacob would tell her in the morning about the Reapers. That they didn't forget and never stopped hunting. He would tell her how far they needed to go to truly be safe. He had never seen one that powerful before. He looked back at Brynn who looked so small under the blanket. She didn't realize how strong she proved to be tonight.

He didn't know when he drifted off to sleep, but he woke up to a very cold breeze across his skin. He rubbed his eyes and reached to pull the blanket up over himself. He looked over to Brynn's sleeping form, but the bed was empty.

He jumped up and scanned the room. Her shoes, bag, and stuff was still there. He looked in the bathroom, and it was empty. He came back into the room and noticed the drapes were moving. He pulled them open and found the window was wedged open with something. He pulled on it and found it was his book he had left at the hospital. His heart started racing. There was something sticking out of the middle of it. It was a lock of Brynn's hair, and in some kind of black substance, it read: "Mine now."

TALIA

Talia awoke to the sound of shattering glass.

Looking down at her wrist monitor, she saw the time. "Shit," she muttered. She was not supposed to have slept for so long.

Scanning the room, she assessed her situation. It was still dark. She could see in low light, therefore her vision wasn't impaired, but she was happy that it wasn't light out yet. It was easier to move and hide at night.

She was happy to find that she was still alone in the room. Her tripwires and traps were all in place. Checking her monitor again, she saw that the other traps and warning systems had not gone off. This was good. Whatever had caused the noise was not within 30 meters.

She closed her eyes and listened for a moment. She had done this exercise often enough that she could slow her breathing and calm herself to focus on what she needed to hear. At first, there was nothing, then faintly in the background, she heard the buzzing. Over time, they had become more streamlined, more silent. However, they always made noise and since she knew what to listen for, she was not surprised.

Listening to the rhythm, she could tell there were two of them. They were almost swerving back and forth. These sounds let her know that their movement was them sweeping the area. They hadn't found her yet.

Then she heard the sound of shattering glass again. They were trying to get her to move, to startle. This tactic would normally work for most people or creatures. Talia, however, was not most people.

As a courier, she would oftentimes have to hide with her cargo. She had gotten used to this and learned early on the Scouts and even the Hawkers had a pattern to their approach. These were Scouts. This also meant they didn't know what they were looking for, just that they were looking for something.

She checked the gauges again on her suit. It was holding temperature. This suit was what truly made the difference for those like her. It was a thin mesh that caused sensors on scouts to detect nothing. Effectively she now matched the exact temperature of the area where she was.

It took training to use the suit. It changed the air temperature into and out of the body to ensure it fully masked any difference. Extreme temperature changes meant she had to train her breathing. Otherwise, she would cough or choke and give away her location. It also meant her skin would constantly adjust to the temperature as well.

Talia had already had other modifications done—her eyes, ears and nose were the first. Enhancing the senses. The latest modification was to desensitize her skin. This meant she didn't feel the same way others did. She didn't need to. Not for the kind of work she did. There was always the promise it could be reversed. She had yet to see this successfully happen. This might have been partially because most people in her line of work didn't live to retire.

She stared at the small metal box before her. It was a six-inch square about four-inches tall.

This was her cargo.

She had taken the job because the request seemed extremely easy for the pay. Looking back, she realized it had been too easy.

Talia had assumed that the job had been posted by a wealthy person for whom price didn't matter. Since she always went through her broker, the Requestor didn't matter. It was all transactional. Once she had taken the job, it had been removed from the listings. So long as she successfully completed it, she would receive the credits.

Most of the time, these jobs were listed to hide something. Maybe there were debts, evidence in a criminal investigation, or an unforgivable tryst gone wrong. It was something that needed to disappear, and they were willing to pay anything to make it happen.

The system was simple enough. This job hadn't been.

Getting to the item had not been the issue; getting out with it had. The item was in a residence. The instructions for how to find the item were very clear. The house had been relatively unprotected, and Talia went in at night so that no alarms could be sounded. She simply assisted the sleeping couple and child to sleep a little deeper. They would not know who had been there.

When she had hit the edge of the city, she thought she was mostly home free. Then the bulletin was released detailing the theft. To her credit, they didn't have her identity or any indication they knew the identity of the perpetrator of the crime. But the item needed to be found. The reward issued was more than the job. If she never wanted to work again, she would have taken it.

Since that night two days ago, she had been on the move as much as possible. It should not take more than three days to get to the drop point, but this was the third safe spot she had to stop in. She had also had to travel through areas that even the Scouts wouldn't normally patrol. The Scouts being here so long, however, meant that they were no longer simply patrolling; they were looking.

She listened again, but the buzzing was gone. Maybe they had given up and moved on to the next spot to check? She moved to quietly undo her equipment; she needed to finish this and drop her cargo. With another two days to go, she knew that it would take its toll on her.

She was coiling up the last of the wires when she heard the faint sound of slithering scales and claws against stone.

It was a Drudger. She slid the coil into her pack and grabbed the box. The sound was closer now. She had to run.

The Scouts hadn't simply left. They were trying to pinpoint. They would only do that kind of chase if they knew the general area where she was. If she had slept a moment longer, she would not have had time to escape.

As she ran, she grabbed a vial from her belt. In a swift practiced motion, she slid it into her neck through the mesh of the suit. She would be able to run for over two hours without stopping. When she did stop, she would need to rest again.

Synthetic stimulant was a help in these situations. But the frequency she was needing it would create a burn-out, or her heart would eventually explode. Neither of these was going to have a positive outcome. Plus, it was eating into her profits.

As she exited the mostly destroyed structure, she assessed her situation again. Although she wanted to be cautious, because of the stimulant, she knew she would not be able to do the same level of stealth she normally had when she wasn't hyped on the juice.

Scanning quickly, she saw that the Drudger was making fast work of the building. In the distance to the north and south, she could see two others. This was bad. She closed her eyes again to focus. She listened, filtering out the sounds of the building falling in behind her. She only had a few seconds but needed to know if the Drudgers had support.

After a moment, the faintest sound of whirring was able to be discerned. She didn't have time to see how many Hawkers were above her. She did know one thing: this job just turned so it was absolutely not worth the fee. She opened her eyes and took a deep breath. The only chance she had was to outrun them.

The results if she didn't would be either bludgeoned to death by the Drudger or ending up a bloodless corpse from the Hawker. They wanted the cargo, not the courier. Keeping a courier alive meant spending time and credits, and the corporation would have none of that.

She pulled down her visor and darted for the nearest shadow. She had to keep moving. She tried to stay out of sight as much as possible, but she could not turn back. She flipped on her forward sensors. With any luck, and she needed luck, she would see any danger in enough time to avoid it.

Throughout the run, she managed to avoid the pursuers. They were close the entire time, but her investments had paid off, and after about the first hour, they lagged behind, then they disappeared from the radar entirely. She neared the end of the two hours and felt her body begin to slow. She needed to find a place to rest and hide.

She saw the last floors of what she assumed had been a high-rise at one point in time. All that remained were the bottom four floors, no windows or doors. She hoped it had a parking garage.

She sprinted to the rubble across the street then pulled out her Mapper. It was a device that allowed a deeper scan. The danger was that it used sonar so some of the machines could feel it. Talia was willing to take the chance.

She scanned the building, and there was an underground parking garage. It looked as though a pack of dogs or something like it had taken up residence on the second level. She would just have to get past them and lower. This was good because they would help her to hide.

Moving into the garage, she found her eye modifications came in handy. It was dark and shining a light would attract attention. She could handle the pack, but it would draw attention of its own. She found the stairwell and began to climb down. She passed many skeletons on her way down. Talia was familiar with scenes like this one. They were most likely heading down for shelter when the bombs hit. What they didn't know was that even if they had made it all the way down, they wouldn't have survived. Nothing had.

She was careful and slow as her body allowed her to go. She was still buzzing, and even as the juice wore off, it was hard to ensure she was quiet enough not to draw company.

When she finally hit the bottom level, the door was open. She looked around and found the shelter that had been built. She also saw the trail of those who were trying in vain to hole up there. She pulled some plugs out of a pouch and stuffed them in her nose. Although she was sure there was nothing left behind the door, she knew that the smell of rot had nowhere to go.

She braced herself and pulled on the door. It didn't open. She looked at the keypad next to the handle. It was still lit. Interesting...

Carefully, she pulled out her tools and did a bypass. She heard the lock click and turn inside the casing. With that, she pulled a knife from her boot and readied herself. She pulled the door open to find a fully lit room with tables to seat about fifty and racks that she had supposed all held food and water for a time that were now mostly empty. There was an opening before her, and she moved toward it, still buzzing.

The room was full of bunks with rolled up mattresses and bags that contained a small pillow and blanket. She scanned again and found no heat signatures. Moving to the back of the room, she found a skeleton on one bunk and a body, mostly decayed, on another. She picked up the ID sitting beside the decaying one. Michael Ashton—CEO—Ashton Enterprises.

He saved himself.

She looked for a badge on the skeleton, but Talia didn't find one. Based on the clothes, it had been female. At least they hadn't had a child down here.

Talia closed the door and found the best place to rest: the opposite corner from the one she had found the body in. She didn't bother moving the body; there wasn't a point. She set an alarm for two hours. It didn't take long for sleep to take her.

The alarm went off, and Talia looked around. She had turned off the lights, so scanning was easy. She was still alone, and there was no sign of Corporation within her scans. She pulled up the wire, a way for communication to flow. She would have about ten seconds to download any messages. She turned it on, counted, and turned it off.

There were two, both from her Broker.

The first was a series of news bytes. The family she had acquired the package from had been slain inside their home. This along with four other families linked to political parties opposed to Corporation rule. She read each one. Talia was the suspect in all cases. Her face was plastered all across them, and the reward for her capture was quadruple the reward for the theft, which was no longer being mentioned.

The second was more ominous. It was her Broker. His name was Jimmy—they were all named Jimmy. He looked stressed; she had never seen any emotion other than boredom on his face even when a gun was pointed at it.

"Drop the package..." He suddenly looked at something off camera. "Hide!" The transmission suddenly terminated.

She took a deep breath.

Pulling out the box, she knew the game had changed.

MITCHEM

I believe almost everyone invariably wonders what happens when we die.

I suppose there are those that "think" they know. Although I don't think most of us think about death unless something happens that calls attention to it, such as old age, having a doctor tell us they need to run some tests because they are not sure what is "wrong," or even having an accident that could have been much worse, but we walked away with only a few bumps and bruises.

In my case, it would be having way too many weapons pointed at me with the threat of said weapons being used if I didn't comply with the request of the person doing the pointing. I of course deemed myself to be a rebel of sorts, and the thought of complying usually never crossed my mind.

So, in those moments, I didn't consider what I thought would actually happen to me after I died. The thoughts that I found myself having were more centered around the actual fact that there was a real threat of death happening to me, and I should be able to avoid it.

Now that it had finally happened, honestly, I was surprised.

Looking at the explosion of cargo ship I had been travelling in as it was being smashed to bits by an uncharted piece of space-rock that it collided with was not how I saw my life ending. Here I was, however, watching it happen.

This perspective only came after the initial moment where my tender fleshy body was rigorously ripped apart as the bulkhead in my quarters folded like a piece of paper. For the record, that was not pleasant and also not as painless as often professed to be.

Now this.

For a brief moment, I wondered if this was truly the end: floating, or at least I assume I am floating, out in space for eternity. That would be a bleak future. I wanted to be outraged.

Since there are so many different religions, beliefs, and mythology on the subject of death, one would assume just based on sheer chance, one of them would have close to the right idea of what happens when the physical form is no longer functioning.

Many believe that where we end up, spiritually, is based on fate. We are ostensibly pre-destined for an amazing afterlife based on who we are in this life. If we are royalty or an important person, such as a celebrity or ruler of some worth, we should continue to maintain this stature when we pass over.

Others would insist our destiny is based on how well we provided to our place of worship before we passed on. The more we donated, the more we will have when we arrive to the other side. Many societies go as far as to bury wealth with their dead. Though there are no recorded stories as of yet which plane the corpse and the wealth ended up beyond the one they were laid to rest on.

Of course, there are those that simply do not believe that anything has a spirit. Everything is simply pieces of sentient matter. They think that the universe just recycles the flesh for the world as it keeps moving.

Humans use the world "Soul" to describe the spiritual part of us, where the Reaken call it something that roughly translates to "bulb of rot in heart" or something that resembles an English dish called "Spotted Dick" which seems tastier than the first. The Reaken also eat their dead as a sign of honor, so I am not sure if that piece is included on the menu.

Then there are the Recyclers. These people believe we keep coming back over and over again. Whether it is because it is simply destined to happen or is part of some machine that is working to keep the universe running. Others have subtly indicated it is because we haven't lived our lives life correctly, and therefore we need to repeat it until we do. This of course explains why some claim to have memories of the past.

Finally, there are those who think that the more we do right in the world, the more we build up some kind of "good points," and that is what guarantees our place in the afterlife.

Almost all of the options, besides of course the Recyclers, indicate that we don't return to the physical plane we started from. That in fact the place we arrive in after is generally considered to be divided into a good place or a bad place where we then live for eternity. This quite frankly seems unfair since most lifeforms live, on average, between twenty to one-hundred-fifty years. I, at this point, had lived 37. Having our forever based on one life seems a bit extreme, especially if we are put into a place where we are tortured forever. What if I was simply a terrible child? There's no chance at redemption?

The tearing apart and destruction of the ship had finally completed. It had been highlighted by several exquisite explosions, validating the death of all those on board. I wondered if I would see any of the passengers or crew floating out here with me. In the same moment, I wished I had a glass of chilled Gin whilst waiting out here. I knew that I was dead, but the idea of comfort still mentally soothed me. Before I could look around for others or a beverage, I suddenly appeared in a room.

At least, I think it was a room. The walls were such a bright white that I could not really tell if there were corners. There was a table amid the space that was a flat grey color and had two identical chairs on either side of the table that matched the grey color perfectly.

When the question of "Where's the door?" popped into my mind, one opened before me, and in walked a man of similar height and build to me. He was so ordinary looking I couldn't form an easy description. He wore a simple grey shirt, pants, and shoes. There was nothing interesting at all about him besides the small device he was carrying.

He looked at me and asked, "Are you Mitchem Carnell Saunders?"

I nodded slowly. Part of me wanted to ask him some questions and challenge him more on where I was, but I found myself less resistant than normal. Plus, no one had called me by full name since I was a child.

"I require an affirmative yes or no, please," he said. His voice was very plain with no inflection to give away his emotional state. Normally suspicious of people, I found I had no apprehension around this person at all.

"Yes," I said before the thought of resisting even crossed my mind. He hit some buttons on the device he was carrying, then gestured toward the table. "Please have a seat, Mr. Saunders."

I looked at him, then back at the table. It took me a moment to realize that I was missing the comforting feeling of being suspicious of my environment and of other people. I found myself wanting to fight against his request, but at the same time, I didn't.

As I moved toward the table, I realized he didn't point at a particular side, so I chose one and sat down.

"Where am I?" I turned to ask as he was sitting himself in the chair opposite me.

He looked down at his device for a moment, then he looked back up at me. "You are in chamber 12." The way he stated it indicated this should mean something to me.

Before I could ask what chamber 12 was or the million other questions that came to mind, I felt the chair I was sitting in begin to get slightly warm, then cool and return to normal before I could even comment on the change. He again did something with his device.

Then the air around me then became very dry and then moist and then returned to normal. "What is happening?" I asked as he focused again on the device.

You might wonder why I was not reacting more panicked in this situation. As the thought occurred to me to perhaps do so, he spoke again, "You have died, Mr. Saunders." He said this as if it explained everything. Which for some reason, I also wanted it to.

"Can you place your hands on the table, please?" I did this, palms flat, without even thinking. My skin felt as if little pins were being pushed against it all over. They were sharp but did not penetrate. This meant they were uncomfortable but not painful.

Again, he typed into the device.

I pulled my hands away and looked around again at the room I was in and then the man before me. "Who are you?" I asked, trying to focus on some part of him that could be interesting or hold my attention. The device was the only thing of interest.

He looked up again from the device. "Mr. Saunders, I can answer, but this will then make the process take longer. We are almost complete." His voice again betrayed nothing.

"Wait... The proc...?" I knew this wasn't a full question as it left my lips, but it was too late.

"This response does not indicate your decision." He closed his eyes briefly. This was the first time I realized he had done this—a blink.

"Do you want me to answer your questions or proceed with the intake process? Please be clear and affirmative in your answer."

I almost asked what the intake process was but caught myself and simply said, "I would like you to answer my questions." He nodded, closed his eyes again briefly, and when they opened, he stated, "Please ask your questions. However, I must limit you to four as we must maintain the schedule."

"Fine!" I said. I was mad as if he had denied me something. Part of me knew that he was not going to fight with me even if I wanted to try. If I did fight, I wasn't going to win anything. With some defeat, I simply asked, "Who are you?"

Blinking once again, he responded, "I am not a who by human standards, as much as a what. I am a recorder of information. I do not have a name but a designation."

This was not exactly helpful, and I had wasted one of the questions.

Looking at him and the device again, I had to hold myself back from blurting out the questions that were racing through my thoughts. In my life, I didn't focus on a limit to information. There was always just one more piece of information that could be gained and used. It was one of the most valuable commodities in the universe. This is what I had dealt in, information, and now I almost needed it in the way I needed to breathe.

I took a deep breath, but it occurred to me this action was symbolic and not possible as I was no longer technically a life form that needed air. Was I a life form at all?

"You said that I was dead. What am I doing in this place with you then?" I was proud of the construct of this question.

His eyes closed for a bit longer this time, and when they opened, he said, "Every living thing in the universe is energy.

There is a finite amount of it, and therefore it is priceless." He was watching my reaction for comprehension, then he continued, "I am here to collect and measure that energy."

"Measure how...?" I stopped myself. I wondered for a moment if he was going to take that as a question or ask me to rephrase. He did neither and continued to wait.

All of the physical mannerisms that I wanted to do, such as run my fingers through my hair or pace the room, were just habits that meant nothing here. I was dead. I wasn't even sure I could pace or if I had hair and yet, I had to consciously not try to do these actions even though I felt I needed them to think.

Two more questions.

I drummed my fingers on the table. I couldn't help myself.

"What happens to me after I am measured by you?" I looked up at him, waiting for the blink again.

He did and answered, "The energy is eventually placed back into the universe."

This statement was simple and irritating. I couldn't demand he give me longer answers, and I knew it was hard to phrase a question that solicited a long answer unless the person was a talker. He was not.

One question left.

I knew this question would not be enough to explain what I felt I needed to know. There was no way to ask what was going to happen after this moment with enough clarity to get the answers I desired.

He seemed willing to sit and wait for the question. I didn't know if I could drag it out enough that he would say something to me, insisting on me asking my final question as if I had some sort of bargaining chip that I could hold him hostage with. He would and most likely could continue with whatever process and did not have to even entertain these questions.

Finally, I relented this pretend stand-off and asked, "Can I choose what happens to me next?"

He didn't blink this time and simply said, "No."

With my questions at an end, he continued whatever he was doing by holding up the device again and scanning me for a moment. Then he put it down on the table and his fingers moved across the screen until a warm yellow light pulsed on the device.

"Thank you, Mr. Saunders," he said and placed the device before me.

I looked down at the device with was roughly the of my hand, black with a small screen in the middle that had symbols that moved across in some sort of scrolling banner. There was etching atop the device with was laid out like a serial number used for cataloging.

I looked back in the direction the door had appeared and saw no outline of it now. I looked to him then and he was sitting perfectly still.

The light on device pulled my attention again as it was pulsing more rapidly.

I reached down to pick up the device, and as I wrapped my hand around it, I felt the warmth and then the pull toward the warmth. I looked back to see him becoming larger. Then nothing.

Serial Number 87G654C9302-88HUM-34274A was then placed into the purification chamber.

DIANA

"**D**id you find it, Officer..." Detective Martin asked, looking up the name tag on the uniform "...Grahams?"

"Yes. It was on the kitchen counter, just like the others," he replied. His eyes looked everywhere but the body in front of them.

Detective Martin noticed Grahams shifting from one foot to the next. "Was there more?" she tried, calming her voice.

"It has rotted," he stated.

She nodded.

She had assumed that would be the case. Unlike the others they had found, this body had time to decay. Normally, they had been found within 48 hours of the death, the killer had made sure of that, but this one had been almost three weeks, guessing by the decomposition.

Detective Martin sighed, then stood up. She was not going to get any more from the bloated corpse of Mr. Alexander Fleming or at least they assumed that was who it was. The face was removed the same as the other victims.

She signaled to the CSI unit that the scene was ready for them and headed to the door, assuming that Officer Grahams would follow.

As she exited the front door, she inhaled a deep cleansing breath. There was still only the slight odor of death this far away from the body, and the cool fall air almost had a calming effect.

She had been correct about Grahams as he was now standing just a bit behind her on the front porch. "Stay until CSI is done and the body is moved," she said, "then secure the place." He nodded and she headed to the station.

As she drove, she took a few deep breaths.

When she hit a red light, she sent a text.

[Another body. I am sorry. Raincheck?]

As she put the phone down, the light turned green. If Robert didn't reply, she wouldn't blame him. Dating her was turning into too many rainchecks in the last few months.

Her phone beeped as she pulled into the station's garage. After she parked, she read the message.

[K]

Damn it, she thought. Sending a "K" was the texting equivalent of "screw off." He had every right to be mad. However, she knew that she couldn't solve this now. She sighed and slid her phone into her pocket.

As she arrived at her desk, the Captain was already waving her over. She dropped her coat on the desk and headed to his office.

As she walked in, she was surprised to see that the Captain already had company. "Detective Diana Martinez, this is Detective Holly Travis."

Detective Travis stood and extended her hand. "Please, call me Holly," she said, smiling.

Diana extended her hand and shook Holly's offered hand. Holly had a firm handshake, not limp or clammy. She wasn't nervous.

The Captain gestured them to both sit. Taking a seat himself, he said, "Detec... Holly," he said, correcting himself, "is here from Atlanta to assist since your partner is out."

Diana's partner was on parental leave. He had just welcomed twin boys two weeks ago and Diana had insisted he take the time. Although she knew he would have stayed on the case, he would have regretted missing this time with his new babies and helping his wife. Her father had always told her to not let the job get in the way of her life. She thought of Robert then and how she was terrible at taking advice.

"Holly recently handled a case similar to yours." The Captain's voice returned her to the conversation.

"Do you think they're linked?" Diana asked, mostly wondering why someone would be sent from so many states away to assist. Holly seemed to be in her mid-thirties, similar to herself. She was also on the tall side as they both seemed close to eye level, and Diana stood about 5'9.

"No," Holly said, shaking her head. "I'm sure you heard of the Miss You killer?" Diana nodded. Miss You would strangle his victims after violently raping them. He would leave a note on the bathroom mirror saying, "Miss You. XOXO" in the woman's lipstick.

"We found him last week," Holly finished.

"Found him?" Diana asked.

"More specifically, we found a suspect with the lipstick tubes from the crime scenes. There were more lipsticks than bodies. Right now, they are trying to find the rest of the victims before they announce it to the press," Holly said, looking down at her hands and back up again.

The motion was so quick but showed Holly was hiding something. She would have to ask about it later as the Captain chimed in, "Detective Travis will be your partner on this. Get her up to speed. She trained with the FBI for a time, and I asked her to join us. We could use the help." The last words held a ton of weight. Diana nodded and gestured for Holly to follow her out of the office.

"That got tense," Holly said as she followed Diana out the door.

Diana sighed. "This one will be you," she said, pointing the desk across from hers.

Holly put her purse and jacket down.

"Who is the suspect?" Diana asked bluntly.

Holly smirked and sat down. "Figured you caught that. He was a cop in forensics. The only evidence we have is the lipsticks, and there are no prints. He is one of the techs that searched the crime scenes. Of course, they were clear. Also, there were eight more lipsticks than bodies. So, he also has a bargaining chip or eight."

Diana nodded. "That sucks. Unfortunately, it is not great here either. That was the reason for it getting tense." She grabbed a file off her desk and passed it over. "How much did you get briefed on before you arrived?"

"Not as much as I would have liked. My lieutenant mentioned a case up in Wisconsin that had a similar pattern of lack of clues and asked me if I would be willing to assist for a few months. I figured it was better than sitting around waiting for the trial. Also, full disclosure: I was taken off the other case. The suspect is my ex-boyfriend. We had only dated for a couple of months, but it doesn't put me in the best light."

Diana knew from the look on Holly's face she had already beaten herself up about that situation and didn't need any further help in that department.

"Well, then let me introduce you to the Jack-O-Lantern Killer." She pointed at the file. "It is called the Ripper for short."

Diana explained as Holly flipped though the file that the first victim had been found on the first of January. At the time, the date wasn't significant, but they had been led to a body on or around 1st and 15th of every month since then with the exception of last month on the 15th when they thought perhaps the killer had taken a break. However, the two discoveries this week on the 1st and today had proved otherwise.

"So, he removes the victim's face after creating a jack-o-lantern of them?" Holly asked as she looked through some of the photos.

"Yes, well he injects them with insulin, putting them first into a diabetic coma, then he cleans the body as well and dresses them. Then he removes the face from the neck to the forehead. They are alive when this happens so they die from bleeding out from the wound to the carotid artery. We are not sure when the pumpkin is created; however, it is always a perfect likeness and it is always lit. With the exception of the one today, it was supposed to be the one on the first I think." Diana sat down.

Holly looked over the photos again. "Why do you think it was missed?"

"My guess?" Diana shrugged. "I think something happened to his messenger."

"Messenger?" Holly asked.

"Each time a kid, a homeless kid, walks into the station with an envelope and hands it to the desk clerk." Diana grabbed an envelope off the top basket on her desk and started to open it.

"That detail wasn't in the file," Holly stated.

"It was left out intentionally. There are leaks, unfortunately, and the kids are our only lead, if you can call it that, to our killer," Diana said as she pulled a few pages from the envelope.

"So, these kids have seen the guy?" Holly asked.

"You assume it's a male?" Diana asked, looking up from the report she was reading.

"Well..." Holly began to say.

"I am teasing. It is a male, average height, brown hair, brown eyes, white. You know, really easy to pick out of the crowd." Diana stood up and grabbed her jacket. "Let's go." She waved the report in her hand. "We actually have a lead."

Holly grabbed her jacket and they headed out.

The Medical Examiner's office was busy. There were people moving from left to right. Diana walked past the desk clerk, who upon seeing who was walking past just shook her head. Holly simply followed her until they walked into an office at the end of a hallway beyond several exam rooms.

A woman in her early forties with her hair in a tight bun wearing blue scrubs sat behind a desk dictating into a microphone. "The wound was caused by a 45-caliber bullet to the right eye near the bottom of..." Her voice trailed off as she looked up to see who walked in.

"Detective Martin," the woman said, standing.

"Evelyn," she said, smiling. "This is my new partner Holly."

Holly reached her hand out as Evelyn did the same. "Nice to meet you."

"You found DNA?" Diana stated, wasting no time.

Evelyn smirked. "I was surprised it took you this long to get here."

"There was another victim," Diana stated.

Evelyn nodded and gestured for both of them to take a seat. Both Holly and Diana complied.

"Yes. There was DNA at the last scene. I was surprised because it was actually left purposefully on the shirt. It was a clear fingerprint in blood." Evelyn seemed to be looking for a specific file from the pile on her desk. When she found the one she was looking for, she opened it, flipping through the pages.

"Here it is," she said, reading down the page. "Brian Anderson." She handed Diana the paper.

"We got him!" Diana exclaimed as she grabbed the page and looked down at the DMV photo of a white male with brown hair and brown eyes.

"Maybe," Evelyn said, sitting back down in her chair.

"Maybe?" Diana asked seeming annoyed.

"Well, your killer has managed to leave perfectly clean crime scenes this entire time, and he happens to leave a clean thumb print over the heart of the victim this time?" Evelyn shrugged "Just something to consider."

Diana nodded as she got up with Holly in tow. "Thanks." Evelyn smiled and waved her out. "Go catch this guy."

Diana pulled out her cell phone before she even left the building, calling the captain and telling him everything she had just learned. When she clicked her phone closed, Holly asked, "What is the plan?"

"Captain is calling in SWAT to meet at Mr. Anderson's apartment. He doesn't want to take any chances." She opened the car door and got inside.

Holly got in and closed the door. "Maybe you don't need my help after all."

"I hate to say it, but I hope so," Diana said, turning the key.

As they pulled up to the address, they saw that the SWAT team had already assembled. The captain wasn't taking any chances.

They both walked up toward the building's front doors. Diana pulled out her badge to show the doorman. He opened the door to allow her and the team following her in. The license said that Mr. Anderson lived on the eighth floor. They pushed the button for the elevator as several members of the SWAT team moved up the staircase.

As the elevator doors opened, Diana began to move in only to realize Brian Anderson was standing right before her.

Diana pulled her gun and pointed it. "Brian Anderson, hands up!"

Brian looked startled, then calmly held his hands up. Diana cuffed him as Holly read Brian his rights. He was quiet until she asked him if he understood his rights and he then only said, "Yes."

When they arrived at the station, Diana put Brian in an interrogation room and went to see the captain.

Diana discussed the interrogation with the captain as Holly listened. The only evidence they had was the finger print. That was not going to be enough to convict Brian. They needed more. They needed him to admit to the crimes. A search warrant was being gathered for his apartment and car with the hopes that they would find more evidence, but a confession would seal the case.

Diana and Holly walked in the room with a file in hand. It contained photos of every victim. Diana sat, taking the lead as Holly stood toward the back of the room behind the perp.

"Do you know why you are here?" Diana asked.

"I assume you think I committed a crime," Brian responded.

"I do," Diana said. "Where were you the week of August 26th through September 3rd?" she asked, leaning back in her chair.

Brian paused, looking down. After a moment, he said, "For part of that time I was in Texas. I believe I flew out the 27th and returned two days ago."

Diana narrowed her eyes and asked, "I'm sure you have proof?"

Brian nodded. "You can check with my office. They will have all of the exact information on my flights. I stayed at a hotel in mid-town."

"What were you doing in Dallas?" Diana asked.

"I am an engineer. I work on MRI machines... For hospitals. I was on a job at Dale Lipshy Hospital for that week,"

Brian explained. "Can I ask why you arrested me?" Brian's voice cracked.

"How about you give me the info on your alibi, then we can discuss why you are here?" Brian paled at her words as she pushed a note pad and pen over to him.

Armed with the information, Diana left him in the room with Holly following.

"I don't understand," Holly said. "There is no way..."

"That he could have done this crime if he was out of town for that long?" Diana asked, interrupting. "No."

She handed Holly the paper. "Check this out while I see if they've found anything at the apartment."

Holly nodded. "Let me know if you find anything."

"Will do," Diana replied as she pulled on her coat again.

As she arrived at the apartment, she could see that they had already dusted for prints in several locations. The photographer was still taking photos when she spotted Evelyn in the kitchen, looking over some papers on a clipboard.

"Surprised you're here," Diana said as she approached, smiling.

"Catching the Ripper? Of course, the brass wants to make sure nothing can be thrown out," Evelyn said, looking down from her notes.

"What have you found so far?" Diana sounded more anxious than she planned.

Evelyn's eyes narrowed for just a moment. "Unfortunately, not much actually. Mr. Anderson lives here with his girlfriend; I believe you met her in the elevator. He has lived here for the last six years. There is no evidence he is the killer."

"His girlfriend?" Diana frowned for a moment.

"The redhead," Evelyn pointed to a photo on a shelf in the small dining area. "She arrived a few minutes before you got here. I believe she was taken to the station."

Diana walked over to the photo. It was Brian and a red-headed woman laughing with a roller-coaster behind them.

She hadn't realized she was staring until she was startled by her phone ringing. She looked at the number, it wasn't one she recognized. "Detective Martinez," she answered.

"Hey, it's Holly. You need to get back here. The alibi checked out."

"Shit," Diana said in a hushed tone as she closed the phone.

Diana reached the station and Holly was waiting for her in the garage. Diana walked up, and before she could say anything, Holly said, "I wanted you to know before we walk in there that Mr. Anderson has an alibi for every one of the murders."

"What?"

"Yeah. I asked his manager to send me proof on the one, and he ended up sending me his schedule for the last twelve months. He was out of town when each of the murders were committed." Holly handed her some papers.

"Does the captain know?" Diana was scanning and seeing that he was in fact out of town when each of the murders took place.

"Not yet. But he wanted an update. Did you find anything at the apartment?"

Diana closed her eyes and took a deep breath. "No."

"What's next then?" Holly asked. She was looking around and Diana assumed she was getting nervous. This wasn't going well.

"Let's talk to the girlfriend," Diana finally said.

"Are you sure?"

"Yep. Let's learn a little more about Mr. Anderson," Diana said as she opened the door.

As they walked in the room, a woman looked up at them. She had been crying. "I don't understand what is happening. Why are we here?" she said, sobbing.

"How long have you and Mr. Anderson known each other?" Diana asked sitting down across from the woman they now knew was Chrissie Parker.

"I… We have been together for about three years now. I am sorry. Why are you asking me this? What do you think Brian did?"

"I am sorry, Ms. Parker. Can we call you Chrissie?" Holly asked.

Chrissie nodded.

"We are just trying to piece together some things. It would really help if you could answer just a few questions for us. Can you help us?" Holly sat in the chair next to Chrissie.

"Yes. I want to help." Chrissie wiped her eyes. "What are your questions?"

They spoke to Chrissie for almost an hour. They learned that she and Brian had been living together for almost two years. They had no pets. They met because Chrissie worked in a local hospital, and Brian had repaired one of the machines there. Brian had two sisters and his parents both lived in the northern part of the state. Brian had no enemies, had worked at the same job out of technical college, and volunteered at the local Boys and Girls club as a mentor. As they were almost done, Chrissie said, "Brian is a quiet guy until you get to know him. I think he needs to trust a person to open up. He was in the system when he was younger."

"The system?" Diana asked.

"Yeah. Brian was adopted when he was three or four. I think that still affects him a little." Chrissie shrugged. "Can I help with anything else?"

"No. You have been great. We will just get an officer to take you home," Holly said as she stood.

"What about Brian?" Chrissie asked as she stood up as well.

"We have a few more questions for him." Diana didn't give a time he would be ready to go.

"I will wait. I don't want to leave him here alone." Chrissie took her seat again.

147

"Okay then. We will let you know when he is ready to go." They left Chrissie to wait.

The captain was waiting for them outside the door. "Please tell me this whole thing didn't just crash and burn?"

"I..." Diana began.

"We have a lead," Holly said, looking at Diana, then back at the captain. "Brian Anderson was adopted. This means he could have had other family."

"It was his DNA, however. His DNA on a person who was killed while he was out of town. Did I miss something?" the captain's tone was less sympathetic.

"No," Diana said.

"Cut him loose before he sues us," the captain said, walking away.

Diana sighed and walked toward the room where Brian was being held. As they walked Brian and Chrissie out to the squad car that would take them back to their place, Holly said, "Again I am very sorry for the trouble. Thank you again for all your help."

"That's okay," Brian said. "I hope you catch the guy."

As the car pulled away, Diana shook her head. "How is this possible? His DNA and fingerprint were clearly at the crime scene. How does that just happen?"

"Wait," Holly said and raced back inside. When Diana finally caught up to her, she was looking through the files.

"What are you looking for?" Diana asked.

"The connection," Holly continued to look until she found something and handed the open file to Diana.

She scanned the file. It was victim number six, an elderly woman named Margaret Brody. She was about to ask Holly when she saw it: Northend Home for Children.

Margaret Brody was a Child Welfare Specialist who had worked at the Home for over 20 years. She had retired about twelve years ago.

Diana picked up another file and began to read through it with Holly doing the same. They were able to find more than half of the victims had a connection to the Home.

In the morning, Diana and Holly made their way to the Home which was located in a large building that looked like an asylum from a horror movie. "I would hate to have grown up here," Holly stated as she walked toward the gates.

"Agreed," Diana said.

When they got to reception, they showed their badges as asked to speak with the person in charge. After a short time, they were led down a hallway to an office near the end. At no time did they see any children.

As the door opened, a very stern looking middle-aged woman was sitting at a desk. The office was spotless. It was also devoid of any color or artwork. The desk was black and the chairs were a darker grey fabric. The woman gestured to the seats before her. "Detectives, how may I help you?" The woman's tone was anything but friendly. There was a sign on her desk reading Matron Winndew.

"Matron Winndew, thank you for seeing us," Diana began. "We are here to ask you about Brian Anderson."

The woman narrowed her eyes. "Do you have a warrant?" she asked, leaning back into her chair.

"No..." Diana began to say, but the woman interrupted, "No warrant, then I am afraid I cannot help you." Then she folded her hands together.

Diana was about to say more, but Holly stood up and put her hand on Diana's shoulder. "Thank you. Matron Winndew," she smiled, "for your assistance."

Holly then turned to exit and Diana followed.

"What in the fu—" Diana began.

"We're not going to get anywhere with her, and plus she is creepy as hell," Holly said as she made her way toward the front desk.

There was a woman who looked up at them, slightly startled by their approach. "Can I help you?" she asked.

Holly smiled at her. "Did you know Brian Anderson?"

The woman took a moment, then said, "Yes and his brother Mark."

"His brother?" Diana asked.

"Yes. They were twins. Although, Mark was a bit more difficult."

"Thank you for your assistance," Holly said, then grabbed Diana by the arm before she could say anything else.

"Why did you pull me out?" Diana asked when they got outside.

"I didn't want what she said to be inadmissible in court," Holly said, smiling.

Diana called the captain on their way back to the station and asked for his assistance in getting the needed warrant.

They looked up Mark Anderson when they got back to the station and could find almost nothing. He was not in the DMV. There was a mention of a Mark Anderson in the juvenile files, but they would again need a warrant for those.

"This is all leading to exactly nothing. It is like he doesn't exist. Do you think we should call his brother?" Holly asked. "Maybe he knows something."

Diana thought about it for a moment, then shook her head. "Not yet." She sighed and rubbed her face with her hands. "What I think is I need some sleep. We will get the warrant in the morning, and we can discern where to go from there."

Holly nodded and they grabbed their coats.

Diana dropped Holly at the hotel and headed to her place. When she got to the door, it was unlocked. She pulled out her gun and pushed the door open, feeling for the light. The switch did not work, and she made her way into the apartment gun drawn.

"Hello?" she said. "This is Detective Martinez. If you are inside, I am armed."

There was no reply.

She made her way down the hallway and saw a dim light in the kitchen. As she rounded the corner, she saw that sitting on the counter was a pumpkin with a carving of her face. She gasped, but before she could react, she felt a needle plunge into her neck from behind.

ERIKA LANCE

Erika had the unique opportunity to live in several different environments across the country growing up, giving her a colorful perspective on life. Born in Minnesota, she spent most of her formative years in Hollywood, then a ranch in New Mexico on the border of an Indian reservation. With a love of the arts since she was a child (acting, painting, sewing and dancing to name a few!) she found her passion in writing. Beginning with short stories, poems and articles for local papers, "Jimmy" is her first published fiction story.

More Erika Lance Books

Illusions of Happiness
No Place for Happiness

Jimmy

Jump: a horror novel
on the **YONDER** mobile app

MORE BOOKS FROM 4 HORSEMEN PUBLICATIONS

HORROR, THRILLER, & SUSPENSE

ALAN BERKSHIRE
Jungle
Hell's Road
Linda's Story
Genocide

MARIA DEVIVO
Witch of the Black Circle
Witch of the Red Thorn
Witch of the Silver Locust
Witch of the White Serpernt
Witch of the Golden Veil

OCTOBER KANE
Nothing Will Be Left
Everything Will Burn

MARK TARRANT
The Mighty Hook

STEVE ALTIER
The Camping Trip
Jimmy's Curse
The Ghost Hunter
Old Man Smithers

PARANORMAL & URBAN FANTASY

AMANDA FASCIANO
Waking Up Dead
Dead Vessel
Dead Show
Dead Revelations

CHELSEA BURTON DUNN
By Moonlight
Moon Bound
White Moon
Blood Thirsty

BEAU LAKE
The Beast Beside Me
The Beast Within Me
Taming the Beast: Novella
The Beast After Me
Charming the Beast
The Beast Like Me
One Mummy To Go, Please!

J.M. PAQUETTE
Call Me Forth
Invite Me In
Keep Me Close
One Mummy To Go, Please!
Heart of Stone

DISCOVER MORE AT 4HORSEMENPUBLICATIONS.COM